LEGAL ATTRACTION

LISA CHILDS

D0543044

MILLS & BOON

First Published in Great Britain 2018
by Mills & Boon, an imprint of HarperCollins*Publishers*
1 London Bridge Street, London, SE1 9GF

© 2018 Lisa Childs

ISBN: 978-0-263-93219-5

MIX
Paper from
responsible sources
FSC˘ C007454

This book is produced from independently certified FSC™ paper
to ensure responsible forest management.
For more information visit www.harpercollins.co.uk/green.

Printed and bound in Spain
by CPI, Barcelona

Special thanks to Megan Broderick—

for keeping me on track for all those things like Dedications and Dear Reader Letters and Art Fact Sheets.

I appreciate all your help!

CHAPTER ONE

DAMN IT! RONAN HALL had been seeing her everywhere. But then, Muriel Sanz was everywhere: on every billboard in Times Square and on the cover of every magazine in every newsstand in the city. Hell, in every city...

Ronan hadn't expected to see the woman here, though, in the lobby of the apartment building he'd just been about to leave. She'd walked in as he'd been walking out, but he'd turned around to follow her to the elevator. Maybe he should have expected her to be here, since he knew *they* were friends. Their friendship could cost him his law license if the bar association believed Muriel's lies and the evidence she'd manufactured against him.

Damn her!

As the elevator doors began to slide closed, he shoved his hand between them and held them open. She wasn't getting away from him. Not that she'd been trying. She hadn't seemed to notice him at all as she passed through the lobby of the building in the Garment District. While crossing the polished terrazzo floor she had been looking down at her cell phone, typing a text.

Who was she texting? Her friend Bette? A lover? Given what he knew about her and her insatiable appetites, probably a lover.

The doors started to close again—on his fingers. He cursed and used both hands to shove them open so he could step inside the car.

She stood alone in the elevator, at the polished brass control panel, pressing the button to shut the doors. She had definitely seen him now. Her naturally tan skin was flushed, and her pale green eyes were bright with anger.

She was so unbelievably beautiful—maybe the most beautiful woman he'd ever seen. That was why she was such a successful supermodel. Her hair had strands of every color in it, and her face was all cheekbones and full lips and those big, beautiful eyes. And her body...

Even though she wore a long, oversize sweater with black leggings, the green knit clung to every swell of her full breasts and curvy hips and ass. It just wasn't fair she had a figure like that.

And he suspected none of it was surgically enhanced or the media would have discovered and had a field day with that, just as they had every other aspect of her life.

That was why he saw her everywhere—even in his damn dreams.

"What the hell are you doing here?" she asked.

He'd been in the building to see her friend Bette Monroe. He and his law partners, minus their managing partner, Simon Kramer, had come to talk to her on Simon's behalf. Bette was Simon's former assistant, and he was miserable without her—personally more than professionally. And it was Ronan's fault that she'd broken off her personal relationship as well as her professional one with Simon.

So, after his partners had left, he'd stayed behind, trying to decide if he needed to come back and apologize to her again. Or maybe for the first time. He wasn't exactly sure if he'd already apologized or not. But then, he wasn't exactly sure if he owed her an apology or not.

"I'm going to see *your friend*," he said, his decision made, and he reached for the control panel.

A button was lit up, but it wasn't for the tenth floor where Bette's apartment was. Before he could touch it, Muriel slammed both her palms against the panel, hiding the buttons but also pressing them all in the process. The doors closed, and the car began to ascend. The elevator was small, with smoked mirrors, polished brass and a floor that matched the terrazzo in the lobby.

"What the hell are you doing?" he asked.

The car stopped and the brass-plated doors slid open. But she didn't step out of the elevator. Instead, she jabbed the button to close the doors again. Then she pressed the button for the lobby, but all the other floors were already lit up. They would have to stop at every one going up before the car would bring them back to the ground level.

"You're not going to harass Bette anymore," she told him. "She is not the one who gave me the evidence I forwarded to the bar association."

"Evidence." He snorted. "That's not evidence. All of it is forged bullshit, and that's going to be easily proven."

Her wide eyes narrowed with suspicion. "If that's the truth, then why are you so tense? So nervous?"

"Because I'm pissed you'd go to such extremes to smear me." A former runaway who'd spent some time living on the streets, Ronan had worked hard to achieve everything he had, and he hated that anything—especially her lies—could put his career and his partners' law practice at risk.

She snorted now. "That I would go so far to smear you? You hired a PR firm to destroy my image! And for what? Just so you would win a bigger settlement for my slimy ex in the divorce?" Her long, thick lashes fluttered, but he doubted she was flirting with him. Was she blinking back tears?

He felt a twinge of something. Sympathy? No. He had none for women like her. The only thing he should feel for her was suspicion and caution. He had no doubt she would try to play him—just like she had her ex-husband when she'd had him sign that ridiculous prenup agreement before marrying him. The only way around it had been to prove who and what Muriel Sanz really was.

The elevator dinged, and the doors opened again. She jabbed the button to close them. "How can you sleep at night?" she asked him.

Not very well lately because he thought of her all the time, even when he was with another woman. He imagined Muriel's beautiful face, her sexy-as-sin body…

How could he be so attracted to a woman like her? What the hell was wrong with his dick?

"I could ask you the same thing," he said. "You're the master manipulator. Is that how you convinced Bette to give you the stationery with the Street Legal letterhead?"

He had started to believe that his partner's former assistant had had no part in Muriel's sick plot. Bette Monroe had seemed stunned when he'd confronted her about her friend filing the complaint with the bar association.

"I told you," she said, slowly, as if he was too dense to understand, "that Bette did not give me anything."

"So you took it from her without her knowledge?" It would have been easy enough to do had she ever visited the offices of Street Legal. But he'd checked, and she hadn't. Maybe Bette had brought some stationery home with her, though. He needed to ask her.

The elevator stopped and the doors opened again.

She jabbed the button to close them. "I did not take a damn thing."

He snorted again. "I'll see if Bette remembers anything." He had already interrogated her once, and of course she had denied helping her friend. But maybe she would remember Muriel going through her purse or taking something from her apartment. Would she admit it to him, though? Or would she continue to protect her friend?

"You and that sleazebag managing partner of yours have already treated Bette like crap," Muriel said. "You are not going to hurt her anymore." Now she jabbed the stop button, and the elevator jerked to a shuddering halt between floors.

"What the hell are you doing?" he asked as an alarm began to ring, echoing throughout the small car. His head started to pound, nearly as hard as his heart had been since the moment he caught sight of her crossing the lobby like she was gliding down a fashion-show runaway.

Ronan was not crazy about confined spaces—especially being confined with her. He punched the button to restart the elevator.

It lurched up, then began to drop—the car and his stomach. He'd been worried about losing his law license, but apparently that wasn't all that Muriel Sanz might cost him. He'd be lucky if he survived this elevator ride with her.

* * *

A scream tore from Muriel's throat as her feet left the floor. The elevator was falling faster than she was, plummeting down the shaft. Then the car jerked so abruptly to a stop that she tumbled forward, falling hard. But she didn't hit the terrazzo floor of the elevator car. Instead she hit a heavily muscled body that had fallen before she had.

Ronan Hall lay sprawled across the car, his legs stretched across the floor while his back and shoulders had slammed against one of the smoked glass and brass walls. Maybe his head had hit the wall, as well, since his eyes were closed.

Was he unconscious?

From where she'd landed against his chest, she stared up at his handsome face. His features could have been carved from granite; he was that chiseled—his jaw square, his cheekbones as sharp as his nose. His lashes were long and thick and black against his cheeks. They didn't so much as flicker.

Despite herself and all the many thousands of reasons she had to hate his guts, concern filled her, and she asked, "Are you okay?"

"I don't know," he replied, his voice low and gruff. "Did we stop falling yet?"

She was afraid to move, just in case they hadn't. That fear was the only reason she lay atop him, her legs tangled with his. Or else she would have scrambled off his body. But she didn't dare in case the elevator began to fall again.

She sucked in a breath and held it, and his scent filled her nostrils and her head. He smelled so damn good—not like expensive cologne that her ex had always worn. No. Ronan smelled like soap and…

A scent that was his alone.

Not only was he handsome as hell but he had to smell good, too? It wasn't fair, but she shouldn't have been surprised. Life had not been very fair to Muriel lately.

She was too positive to let that keep her down, though. She would not stay down now, either, once she was certain the elevator wasn't going to drop all the way to the bottom of the shaft and crumple like an aluminum can under a car tire.

"Are *you* okay?" Ronan's voice, even deeper with concern, asked the question now.

She glanced up at his face to find his eyes open as he studied her. She shrugged, then gasped as the car creaked. Ronan's strong arms slid around her, holding her still—or maybe she had already tensed because he'd touched her. Either way, she was frozen with fear—of falling and of how he was making her feel.

"Don't move," he said, his voice dropping so low that it was a deep rumble in his chest.

She had no intention of moving, but she couldn't control the frantic beating of her heart. It was pounding so hard that she felt her whole body shaking with the force of it. Hers wasn't the only one. His heart hammered in time with hers. Her breasts were crushed against his muscular chest.

"Can I breathe?" she asked, her lungs aching as she tried to control the panic making her want to pant for air.

"I don't know if we should…" he murmured, but his breath stirred her hair as he whispered the words.

A strand tangled in her lashes, but she didn't dare reach up for it. But that meant her hands stayed where they were, and she only just realized exactly where they were and what she was touching. Instinctively she'd extended them to break her fall, and since she'd fallen on him, her hands were on him. One was against his biceps while the other was braced on his thigh. Both muscles rippled beneath her touch, as if he'd just realized where she was touching him, too.

And his body, which had already been taut with tension, grew harder yet. Against her abdomen, she felt his erection straining the fly of his dress pants.

He must have come right from the office to see Bette, since he was still wearing a suit. In the pictures she'd seen of him in his downtime, he'd had on jeans and a T-shirt. Not that she'd seen that many pictures of him in his downtime. If he and his partners in the Street Legal law practice hadn't been as notorious as they were in Manhattan, he probably wouldn't have been photographed at all. But he and the others were infamous for being ruthless litigators and lovers. When they were photographed outside the courtroom, they were usually with a famous female—an actress or model or fashion designer...

She tried to shift her hips, so her mound wouldn't press so tightly against his cock. But he groaned. And one of his arms slid around her back as his hand grasped her hip.

Through gritted teeth, he warned her, "Do. Not. Move."

The elevator had stopped dropping. It had even stopped making those ominous creaking noises. "I don't think it's going to fall," she said.

"I'm not worried about the elevator," he replied.

"Then why are we lying on the floor afraid to move?" she asked.

He groaned again and his fingers tightened their hold. But she doubted that he was in any real pain—because his mouth curved into a slight, naughty grin. "Maybe I was just enjoying you throwing yourself at me."

She sucked in a breath of shock and wriggled, trying to move off him. But his hands held her too tightly, and all she managed was to grind her hips against his groin. And to rock the elevator again.

The cables creaked. But they held. The car was not going to tumble any farther down the shaft. She was not worried about dying anymore. Instead, she was worried about her reaction to Ronan Hall.

Instead of slowing down, her heart was beating

even faster. Her skin was tingling and hot everywhere her body was in contact with his—which was pretty much everywhere. He was so muscular, so tall and broad.

And when she'd sucked in that breath, she'd inhaled his scent again; it filled her head. The way he would fill her...

His erection was so long and hard. Heat rushed straight to hrt core, making her hot and wet. For him?

No. It wasn't possible. She could *not* be attracted to the man who had destroyed her reputation, and nearly her career and her life, as well.

"Let me go!" she demanded.

"Where are you going?" he asked. "We're stuck in an elevator. So we might as well make the most of this opportunity." The hand not clutching her hip slid up her back to her head, which he held in his palm while he pressed his mouth to hers.

As their lips connected, Muriel felt a jolt she wanted to attribute to shock. But she knew it was something else—something that had her nipples tightening and heat streaking to her core: lust.

He kissed her tentatively, at first, just skimming his lips across hers. Then she gasped at another jolt of desire, and he deepened the kiss, sliding his tongue inside her mouth. His kiss was hot, passionate and wild.

And that was how it made Muriel feel: hot, passionate and wild. She didn't want to desire this man, of all men. But he was so damn good-looking—not to mention muscular and skilled.

He was a master kisser—so good that he nearly made her come with just a kiss. But then he began to touch her, too, moving his hand from her hip up her side to cup a breast.

She sucked in a breath, which pushed her breast against his palm.

He gently squeezed, and her breath hissed out between their melded lips. And he groaned in response. He pulled back slightly and moved his hand to the buttons on her sweater, easily flicking them open.

She wore a camisole beneath the sweater. But it was one of her friend's designs, so it was super sexy with bows holding it up at the shoulders. Once he'd pushed the sweater from her shoulders, he reached for one of those bows.

If he pulled it loose, the camisole would slip down, would reveal her breast for him to see and touch…

She wanted his hands on her. She wanted him.

But she couldn't. Not really. Not after what he'd done to her—to her reputation, to her savings and to her sense of self-worth.

The only way she wanted Ronan Hall was…on his knees begging for her forgiveness. And she knew that wasn't very damn likely to happen. Ever.

Not until she'd inflicted the same hell on him that he had put her through.

CHAPTER TWO

RONAN'S HEAD SNAPPED back with the force of her slap. But he only grinned. Even though his cheek was stinging, that kiss had been totally worth it. He could taste her still on his lips. She was so damn sweet.

How could she taste so sweet when she was such a hard and vicious woman? Yeah, he'd needed that slap to bring him to his senses before he did something stupid, like pull that bow loose on her shoulder.

What would she do if he did that? Slap him again? Seeing her without the camisole, that would undoubtedly be worth another slap, though. He could see her tightened nipples pushing against the thin silk. She wore nothing beneath that camisole but her honey-toned skin. He wanted to close his lips around one of those distended nipples and tug at it until she cried out and begged for more.

His fingers still on that bow, he toyed with the end of it. One tug was all it would take.

But then she smacked his hand away and shoved him back with her palm against his chest. "Don't you dare!"

"Don't dare me," he advised her. He was the kid

who would have stuck his tongue on the icy flagpole with the first dare. He wouldn't have even needed to be double dared. He lifted his hand toward her shoulder again.

She jerked up her sweater and wrapped it tightly around herself, as if he would have forcibly undressed her. As if anyone would need to. On all those billboards and magazine covers, she wore barely more than her seductive smile. Usually just a few scraps of lace or silk.

"What game are you playing?" he asked her. She was not a modest woman, but she was a cunning one. Those forged documents proved that. "Game?" she asked, her husky voice pitched higher than usual with outrage. "You're the one who kissed me."

"You trapped us in this elevator and climbed all over me," he pointed out. Was she trying to seduce him? Or just sexually tease him into madness?

"I fell on you," she said. "And *I* did not trap *you*."

He snorted. "I wasn't the one playing with the control panel, punching in every damn floor before you stopped it entirely."

"I stopped it," she said, "because I wanted to stop you from harassing Bette anymore."

"I'm not going to harass Bette," he said. For one— Simon would kill him if he did. The guy was already furious with him over some things Ronan had said to her. Poor Simon had fallen hard for his mousy former assistant.

But then, maybe Bette wasn't that mousy—to a guy who liked the sexy librarian type.

That wasn't Ronan's style. He didn't want someone repressed. He wanted someone as wild and adventurous and as into sex as he was.

Muriel stepped in front of the elevator doors, as if she could stop him. "No. You're not talking to Bette at all anymore."

He didn't want to talk to Bette. He didn't want to talk at all. He wanted Muriel back in his arms, her body pressed to his. She was the one, the female who might finally match his appetites in the bedroom and wherever else they might dare to do it…

"We're stuck here," he reminded her. And as he said it, the elevator rocked and creaked.

And Muriel gasped and shot forward—straight into his arms.

"Did you fall again?" Ronan teased her. "I wouldn't think a supermodel would be as clumsy as you are."

Despite glaring at him, she remained in his arms with hers locked around his shoulders. "Didn't you feel that? We're falling again."

"I've never fallen before," he told her. "So I'm not about to fall now…" And especially not for a man-eater like Muriel Sanz.

Then he realized what she meant even before she murmured, "I was talking about the elevator." Then she started laughing, and as she laughed, she stepped back and dropped her arms from around his shoulders. "I wasn't talking about falling for you. You can't believe I would actually fall for *you*."

He narrowed his eyes and glared at her. She made it sound ridiculous that she could care for him. Plenty of other women claimed that they had. But then, he hadn't had the relationship with those other women that he had with her. Actually, he hadn't ever had a real relationship with anyone.

Just sex…

And he would like to have that with her, even though she was trying to destroy his career. Because from that kiss, he knew it would be good between them. Hell, it would be better than good; it might be great.

He hadn't had great in a while—probably because every time he'd been with a woman the past few months, he'd imagined that woman was Muriel and he'd been disappointed when he'd realized she wasn't.

"I would never make the mistake of thinking you could love me," he assured her. "I don't think you're any more capable of really falling in love than I am."

"I was married," she said, "until you ended that."

"You ended that with your cheating."

She lifted her hand, but before she could swing it toward his face, he caught her wrist. Through gritted teeth, she told him, "I did not cheat."

He snorted again, almost amused over her show of righteous indignation. She could be one of those models who easily crossed over into acting; she had the skills. "So how did your ex find so many witnesses who testified otherwise then?"

Her green eyes widened. "My ex…? He found the witnesses? I thought you did—you or that PR firm."

"Yeah, that was your second mistake when you forged those notes that supposedly came from my case files," he said. "You made it sound as though I found the witnesses." He shook his head. "And that wasn't true."

She glared at him. "What those witnesses said wasn't true. They perjured themselves and you knew it."

"And that was your first mistake," he said. He stepped closer now, pressing his chest up against her breasts. "Trying to blame me for your bad choices."

"Bad choices?" she repeated. "My only bad choice was getting married in the first place."

He nodded. "In that, we are in complete agreement. Marriage is always a mistake." His parents' marriage had showed him that. Their constant fighting was why he'd run away from home for a while in his teenage years. "People aren't meant to be monogamous."

"Many people are," she said.

He shook his head now. "Not people like you and me, Muriel." He skimmed his fingertips along her jaw, down her throat to push her sweater from one shoulder. Then he toyed with that bow again. He was so tempted to tug it loose. So damn tempted.

His fingers twitched and the bow began to loosen. Then the elevator dinged and the doors slid open.

Muriel stepped back through the doors. But as she did, she reached out and struck a button on the control panel. The doors closed as she turned and ran down the hall.

Ronan wasn't sure what floor they had stopped on, or if it had even been her floor, or if she had just really wanted to get away from him. Before he could look at the numbers above the doors, the elevator began to move again—heading down—until it stopped in the lobby.

He hesitated a moment before he stepped through the open doors. He'd changed his mind about trying to apologize to Bette again. It was probably better for Simon if Ronan didn't talk to her at all. He suspected she'd already told him all that she knew. No. If he wanted to get to the bottom of the documents that had been given to the bar association, he needed to talk to Muriel again. But he would have to do that another time—because if he tracked her down now, after that kiss and seeing her nipples pushing against that camisole, he would do a hell of a lot more than talk to her.

Legs trembling, heart pounding, Muriel leaned back against her apartment door. She'd turned the deadbolt, so even if he'd followed her, he would not be able to get inside her place. But she didn't think he'd followed her. The elevator doors had closed before he'd had a chance to step through them.

But he could track her down…especially now that he knew where she'd moved after the divorce. While the building was nice, her apartment was small—much smaller than her old place. Maybe Ronan didn't realize she lived here; maybe he'd thought she was just visiting Bette.

Then she should have gotten off on another floor… because she wouldn't put it past him to knock on every door until he found her.

He was furious with her for reporting him to the bar association. Why was he so angry? Because he'd been caught? Or because he hadn't suborned perjury, as he'd tried to claim?

She could understand his anger if he'd done nothing wrong. That was how she'd felt over her divorce proceedings. She'd been maligned in court and in the media, and she hadn't done anything of which she'd been accused. She had definitely not cheated.

She'd taken her vows seriously. She'd been monogamous. That was all she knew. Even before she'd gotten married, she'd never dated more than one man at a time. And since the disastrous divorce, she hadn't even started dating again.

Maybe that was why Ronan Hall had affected her so much. Or maybe it hadn't been him at all. Maybe it had been the elevator malfunctioning and making her fear that they were about to plunge to their deaths. With her emotions so heightened, it was no wonder she might feel attracted to him.

And it wasn't as if he wasn't good-looking and sexy...

But still, she should hate him, not desire him. And she did hate him.

But what if he *wasn't* responsible for those witnesses coming forward? What if those memos from his Street Legal law practice had been forged, as he'd claimed?

No. She couldn't believe that. She knew every one of those witnesses who'd testified. While they hadn't all been close friends of hers, they were acquaintances. They wouldn't have lied about her without some serious coercion. Arte wouldn't have done that. He hadn't been the man she'd thought he was, but he wasn't a monster or she wouldn't have married him in the first place. He'd once been so sweet and charming.

No. Ronan Hall was the monster. And she would prove it. In case those memos weren't sufficient evidence, though, she needed to find more.

Ronan had been attracted to her, too. And she didn't think it was because he'd been scared. No. He was attracted to her because of how she looked. Her looks were why—despite her reputation being smeared—her career hadn't suffered like she'd worried it would. Magazines and designers said she sold copy and clothes, maybe even more so since she had become so notorious.

But she hadn't wanted to be notorious. And she was mortified that so many people believed those lies about her and that her grandparents—the sweet couple who'd raised her—had heard those lies. About affairs and orgies and sex parties…

While they knew her too well to believe them, they had to contend with the comments from their friends, from their fellow parishioners, from their neighbors…

That was why she hated Ronan Hall. Not so much for what he'd done to her as for what he'd done to them. She wanted him to suffer like they had. That was why she'd turned those papers she'd received over to the bar association. But maybe she should have had them authenticated first. She'd thought Bette had given them to her, though.

But Bette hadn't known anything about them.

So who had delivered that envelope of memos to Muriel's door? And were they real?

She needed to know the truth. And she needed proof of it. The best way to do that was to go directly to the source: Ronan himself.

Could she use her looks to get him to admit to what he'd done? An audio recording of his confession would be indisputable evidence.

But what would she have to do that would compel him to confess? Seduce him?

Instead of disgusting her, the way the idea should have, she was strangely excited by it. Maybe that was just because it had been so long since she'd been with anyone but her vibrator. While that eased some of her tension, it wasn't like being with a man—like having his hands and his mouth on her.

Like Ronan's mouth had been on hers…

Heat flashed through her, and she headed toward her bedroom—and to the vibrator she kept in the table beside the bed. For tonight, it would have to do…while she planned how to seduce Ronan Hall into confessing to his misconduct during her divorce proceedings.

That was what she really wanted. His confession. Not him…

But she thought of him as she pulled the vibrator from the drawer. From the erection she'd felt straining against his dress pants, she knew he was bigger than her toy. And if it was possible, maybe harder…

He had wanted her. No matter how much they detested each other, they couldn't deny the attraction between them. And Muriel would use that to her advantage, just like she used thoughts of him as she shrugged off her sweater and pushed down her yoga pants. Then she lay back on the bed, and she imagined Ronan kissing her, touching her…

She tugged one of the bows of her camisole free and began to touch herself. There were two more bows holding her panties together. She undid those as she flipped the switch for the vibrator. And she imagined it was Ronan's long, hard cock as she slid it inside herself.

She came almost instantly, and to her horror, she cried out his name.

CHAPTER THREE

LIGHTS BLAZED, BUT that wasn't what had sweat beading on Ronan's brow. The heat flashing through him had nothing to do with the lights and everything to do with the woman posing beneath them.

She wore so very little on her gorgeous body—just some scraps of lace and silk and all that naturally tan skin. Desire slammed through Ronan with a force he'd never felt before. It knocked him back on his heels while making his cock rock hard.

Maybe coming here had been a bad idea.

But he wanted to come—inside her. He knew she was the only one who could relieve the unbearable tension that had been building in his body since he'd been trapped in the elevator with her a couple of nights ago.

"Muriel!" the photographer shouted at her. "You're not giving me what I want!"

She wasn't giving Ronan what he wanted, either—because he wanted her to untie that bow between the cups of her strapless black bra, wanted her to untie the bows on each hip that held up her panties.

But he wanted more than to see her naked. He

wanted to feel her, taste her…and bury himself deep inside her.

Why the hell was he so attracted to this woman? He would have screwed her in the elevator if she hadn't pulled away and slapped him. But she'd kissed him back before she'd done that. Was she attracted to him, too?

He was counting on it—so that he could get the truth out of her. That was really why he was here, why he'd tracked her down at her photoshoot. It wasn't for sex.

He could get that anywhere. It wasn't as if he wanted or needed only her. Any woman would do.

No. What he really wanted from Muriel Sanz was the truth.

Her lips curved into a slight smile. "What do you want, Lawrence?"

"Bad," the photographer shouted back. "I need you to be bad."

She was bad, and Ronan had proved that in court. She claimed those witnesses had been lying, though. Why would they lie? Why would they risk perjury charges? They'd had nothing to gain from their testimony.

Muriel Sanz was the liar. And Ronan intended to prove it. He just had to get her to admit to forging those memos. Could he seduce her into a confession?

Those witnesses had claimed she was addicted to sex and that was why she'd cheated on her husband.

So if she was addicted to sex, maybe he could get her addicted to sex with him—so addicted that she would confess all to him.

He knew it was possible for a person to get addicted to another person. That had been his father's downfall: his addiction to Ronan's mother despite how badly she'd mistreated him. She'd been a lot like Muriel Sanz—beautiful and selfish and completely devoid of a conscience.

"I need you to be the badass of Bette's Beguiling Bows," Lawrence said.

This photo shoot was for the line of lingerie Muriel exclusively modeled. That line had been designed by her friend and Simon's former assistant, Bette Monroe.

He had to admit that Bette had a talent for design. Her lingerie was the sexiest he'd ever seen.

Unfortunately, so was Muriel.

"Oh, I can be a badass," she assured the photographer. But she was looking at Ronan now. He could feel her gaze on him, and his skin began to heat even more. She raised her husky voice a little more, probably making certain he would hear, and added, "I can be very, very bad…"

Ronan chuckled. She'd already started confessing…and he hadn't even touched her yet.

The camera clicked.

She ran her fingertips down her deep cleavage to the bow between her breasts. And she toyed with the ends the way he'd toyed with the bow the other night…in the elevator.

Too bad that bow hadn't been between her breasts, too. Then he could have touched her, like she was touching herself.

As she stroked her fingertips up and down her cleavage, she sank her teeth into her bottom lip then swiped her tongue across it.

And Ronan groaned. The photographer echoed the sound and shot a glance at him. Instead of admonishing him for trespassing on the set, the guy grinned at him. "You must be the reason for that sudden spark in her eyes," Lawrence said. "You made her bad."

Ronan chuckled. "Nobody made Muriel that way." Least of all him. She'd already been bad.

"I'm good," she said. And she tilted her head provocatively. "Very, very good…"

And both men groaned again.

Lawrence muttered, "Now I understand why her ex…"

"What?" Ronan asked when the guy trailed off. "Why he what?" Divorced her or married her?

The photographer just shook his head. "You can stay," he told Ronan. "But don't distract me."

"What about me?" Muriel asked.

"He's a good distraction for you," Lawrence said.

Could he be? Could Ronan distract her enough that she would withdraw her complaint to the bar association?

He had to try, at least. That was why he was here. That and the fact that thoughts of her and that damn kiss had been keeping him awake.

He wanted more than a kiss.

He was not a good distraction for her. But as Muriel peered over Lawrence's shoulder at the computer monitor at the thumbnails of all the photos the photographer had taken, she couldn't deny that Ronan had certainly inspired her. This was by far the best shoot she'd ever had and she had been modeling since she was fourteen years old—more than a decade.

"If you're not going to take that man out for a drink, I will," Lawrence said. "He got you to the money shots, baby!" He turned around and kissed her lips. "You have never looked more gorgeous!"

Muriel chuckled at the photographer's enthusiasm. "I'm sure he's already gone."

She couldn't imagine why he had showed up to begin with…unless he was after the same thing she was.

The truth…

He probably wanted to know how she'd gotten her hands on the memos she'd turned over to the bar association. At least he must have finally accepted that Bette hadn't given them to her. That was good. She never would have used them had she known the problems it would cause for her friend.

"I'm still here," a deep voice murmured.

That was not good.

She glanced up to find his long, muscular body leaning against the doorjamb of Lawrence's office. He was wearing a suit; he must have come either straight from the office or from court. Who else's life was he ruining?

She was afraid it might be hers again if she dared to try her plan to seduce him into a confession. Could she take the chance?

"I can leave," he offered, "if I'm interrupting…"

"You interrupted the shoot," she said. "And you didn't offer to leave then." Hours ago. He had stayed through changes in wardrobe, hair, makeup and backdrops.

Why had he stayed so long?

"He improved the shoot," Lawrence said. "Your best work ever…" He turned back to the computer monitor with all the frames and murmured, "Maybe mine, too."

A little thrill chased through Muriel, but she worried it had less to do with the praise than with how Ronan was looking at her, with how he'd been looking at her the past couple of hours. With every wardrobe change, his eyes had gotten darker and his body even more tense. Despite the way he was leaning now, she could feel that tension; it fairly radiated from him.

So that she felt it, too—coiling low in her body, pulsing in her clit. She couldn't remember ever wanting a man more, which was crazy. She had been in love before and hadn't felt this powerful attraction. But this man—this man she hated—she wanted more than any other.

Maybe she had lost her damn mind. That was the excuse she was going to use for what she was about to do. "So, how about it?" she asked as she walked toward the doorway. "Do you want to go for a drink?"

His dark eyes narrowed as if he was as suspicious of her offer as she was of his showing up at the photo shoot. Now a little chill moved through Muriel, raising goose bumps on her skin despite her having changed into street clothes of jeans and a sweater. She hadn't felt a chill like this when he'd been staring at her, when she'd been wearing nothing more than a bra and panties. Then she had felt hotter than hell. And it showed in those photos.

But wondering how he'd tracked her down unnerved her. How had he found her?

She hesitated as she neared the doorway where he stood. But then he stepped back into the hall. "I didn't come here just to watch," he said. "That's not my thing…"

She narrowed her eyes with suspicion. Was it just that everything he said sounded like sexual innuendo or was he actually implying that there was something between her and Lawrence?

Of course, he had seen Lawrence kiss her. But Lawrence kissed everyone. *Everyone.*

"Good night," she called back to the photogra-

pher. He barely glanced up from the computer monitor to wave.

As she walked down the hall of the old warehouse,
she turned to Ronan and asked, "Why did you come
here? And how did you find me?"

"I have my sources," he said.

And that chilled her blood even more. "I am well
aware of that," she said. "But I can't believe they actually got it right this time."

He stopped at the elevator and turned toward her,
his dark eyes narrowed. "So all those witnesses were
lying and you're the only one telling the truth?"

"Yes," she said. Her grandparents had raised her
with values—one of which being that it was never
okay to lie, not even little white ones. Too bad those
witnesses hadn't been raised the same way she had.

"Why would everyone else lie?" Ronan asked her.

"You tell me," she challenged him. "Did you pay
them?" He must have. What else could they have had
to gain, except for some time in the horrible spotlight
that the scandal had shone on her?

He chuckled. But he didn't answer her question.
He just turned and pressed the button for the elevator.

What would it take to get him to confess to somehow coercing those witnesses into lying? He was rich.
So he didn't need money. He had probably used his
own to pay them off since Arte hadn't had much
money until he'd taken most of her savings—and the

apartment and car—in the divorce. He didn't even know how to drive.

The elevator dinged, and the doors slid open with a swoosh of noise and air. Muriel sucked in a breath at the thought of getting into another elevator with Ronan Hall.

He stepped back and waited for her to pass through the doors in front of him. "Come on," he said. "As long as you don't mess with the control panel this time, we'll be fine."

She hesitated. "We could take the stairs…" It would probably be safer—for a few reasons.

"We're on the twelfth floor," he reminded her. "Did you take the stairs up?"

"No."

"So you don't have a problem with using the elevator," he said as if he was cross-examining her again, the way he had on the witness stand. "You just have a problem with taking the elevator with me."

While his cross-examination had been ruthless, he hadn't shaken her. But then, she'd had the resolve of the truth on her side. He didn't have that, so maybe she could shake him. But she was not going to get a confession out of him unless she was alone with him. Dare she go through with her plan? Dare she be alone with him?

Because she knew what was going to happen…

The attraction between them was too strong—

so strong that it could probably even overpower the anger and resentment and distrust between them.

She stepped into the elevator car. And when she automatically reached for the control panel, she pulled her hand back to her side. She was not going to risk getting stuck with him again.

He chuckled as he stepped inside with her. Then he reached for the panel. She didn't see which button he pushed; she just assumed it was for the lobby. In the heart of the Garment District, the building's tenants were mostly fashion designers along with a few photographers. There was no place to have a drink there.

Muriel really needed that drink. Hell, she needed more than a drink. She couldn't remember the last time she'd eaten. And she was not the type of model who starved herself. She enjoyed food too much.

Fortunately, the fashion industry appreciated curves now over skin and bones. Or she wouldn't have been able to get any work. Now she was sought after...

Professionally. Personally—not so much. Men weren't eager to date the man-eater the media had painted her as being. She'd overheard people talking about how she was too intimidating to the opposite sex now.

Ronan Hall hadn't appeared too intimidated the other night. And he must not have been or he wouldn't have sought her out again.

The doors closed, shutting them into the stark car

together. This elevator wasn't nearly as fancy as the one in her building; it was all bare metal and wood, and it was bigger—big enough to carry crates of garments from one floor to the next.

She didn't have to stand anywhere near Ronan. But it didn't matter how far away she was from him; she could feel his presence. It was as if electricity arced between his body and hers.

Her skin tingled, and her blood heated, pumping hot and fast through her veins. "We should go somewhere with a kitchen," she said. "I'm hungry, too."

She felt a hollowness inside, but she wasn't sure that it was one food could fill. Maybe only he could…

He reached for the panel again, jabbed a button and the elevator shuddered to a stop.

"I'm hungry, too," he said as he reached for her. He wrapped his arm around her waist and reeled her in until her body pressed against his. He was so big, so broad, so tense.

His erection strained against his pants—and against her hips. Instinctively she arched and rubbed against him, and he groaned.

"And with every outfit you changed into, I got hungrier," he said.

"You didn't have to stay." But she'd been glad that he was still there—every time she had stepped out of the dressing room after a wardrobe change. She'd wanted him to see what she was wearing; she'd wanted him to see her, and she'd wanted to see his reaction.

"I couldn't leave," he said, his voice gruffer now as if he was in pain.

"Why not?" she asked.

"Because I didn't get what I came for…"

"And what did you come for?" she asked.

He lowered his head to hers and kissed her—deeply—hungrily. His lips moved over hers, nibbling and plucking at them until she gasped with pleasure.

"I came for you," he said, his voice a gruff whisper. "I came for this…"

His hands moved over her, lifting her sweater up and over her head. He uttered a lustful sigh. "I was hoping you were still wearing this…"

It was the black bra with the bow in the middle. Bette was a genius designer. She somehow made the bras so that the one bow held the cups together and provided support. Muriel's breasts swelled over the top of it.

"Why?" she asked, and she wasn't faking the breathlessness in her voice. Her heart was racing so fast that she could barely draw any air into her lungs. But as she tried, her breasts swelled even more and nearly spilled over the top of the black bra.

Ronan reached for that bow, tugging on the ribbons, and the bra fell away, freeing her breasts. She panted for air now as excitement coursed through her. Her nipples tightened and ached for more than the touch of his gaze.

"That's why," he replied. "I've been dying to undo that bow."

Muriel had been modeling lingerie and swimsuits for most of her career, so she had long ago gotten over any qualms she might have had about modesty. But there was something about the way that Ronan Hall was looking at her that made her feel more naked than she had ever felt before.

He wasn't just looking at her body. It was as if he was trying to peer into her heart and soul. Maybe he was wondering if she had one.

She did. She doubted that he did, though. So what the hell was she doing getting half-naked in an elevator with the man who had nearly destroyed her?

CHAPTER FOUR

RONAN'S HEART POUNDED in his chest and in his cock. He couldn't believe how damn beautiful she was. Her breasts were full and perfect mounds, her nipples ripe and rosy. He wanted to close his lips around one so badly. But when he reached for her, she stepped back.

Her green eyes widened with panic and she lifted her hands to cover her breasts.

He glanced around the elevator. Was there a security camera in it? He hadn't thought about that, although he should have. But after watching that photo shoot, he hadn't been able to think at all. He had only been able to feel, the desire coursing through him.

He wanted her more than he could remember ever wanting anyone else. He wanted to become an addiction for her, but now he was afraid that it might be the other way around—and that was before he'd even had her.

Maybe this was a mistake. Maybe he should be taking a step back like she had. He felt a punch of the same panic he saw on her face. But it wasn't nearly as strong as the punch of desire that had his stomach tightened into knots.

"What the hell are we doing?" she asked, her voice shaking with horror.

He shrugged. It wasn't as if he could admit to wanting to seduce her into telling the bar association the truth. She might not even know what the truth was anymore. His mother had gotten that way—so caught up in her own lies that she'd begun to believe them.

"I hate you," she told him, her voice shaking with anger. "I hate what you did to me."

And now he felt another kind of punch—of regret. But he'd only been doing his job—getting the best deal for his client. "*I* didn't do anything…"

…That she hadn't had coming. She'd put her husband through hell. He hadn't seen a man that broken since his father. He flinched as he felt that jolt of panic again. But he didn't have to worry. He wasn't like her ex or his father; he was too smart to fall for a pretty face. Hell, he was too smart to fall for any face. Ever…

Her breath hissed out between her teeth. And she leaned down to grab her bra up from the floor of the elevator. "How can you say you didn't do anything? You hired a PR firm to smear me!"

"It's not like your career suffered for it," he pointed out. "In fact, I think the whole trial helped your career." Now everyone knew her name and her face, whereas before they might have only known her body. While she had been modeling lingerie and swimsuits for years, she hadn't become famous until her divorce drama.

She shook her head, and her titian hair swirled around her bare shoulders. She had yet to put on the bra. She still held her arms across her breasts.

He wanted to see them again. He wanted to touch them. Taste them…

"You should be thanking me," he said, grinning as he goaded her.

She lifted one hand away from her breasts to swing it toward his face. But before her palm could connect, he caught her wrist and jerked her body against his.

"That's not how you thank someone," he admonished her. And he lowered his face to hers. "This is how you thank someone…" The minute he touched his lips to hers, he forgot all about teasing her. Or the panic he'd felt.

He forgot everything but how much he wanted her. Her soft breasts pushed against his chest, and he could feel the tightness of her nipples through the thin silk of his dress shirt. He swallowed a groan as his body tensed and throbbed with desire. Then he swallowed her moan when a soft one slipped through her parted lips. He deepened the kiss.

He slid his tongue inside her mouth, and she stroked hers over his. They mated and tangled around each other, teasing, tasting…

It was the hottest kiss he'd ever had—all panting breath and moans. It was wet and wild. And he wanted her the same way. He wanted her wet and wild for him. So he eased her body back from his, and he touched her.

He moved his hands over her beautiful breasts, skimming his fingertips over her silky soft skin before stroking them over her tightened nipples.

She moaned again.

Then he lowered his head to her breasts and he replaced his fingers with his lips, closing them over one of those taut nipples. He gently tugged, teasing her.

Her hands slid into his hair, grasping his head. But she didn't pull him away. She clutched him closer. Her fingers moved from his head to his neck, and she jerked his tie loose before tackling his buttons. Once she parted his shirt, she raked her nails down his chest.

His stomach clenched as desire punched him hard in the gut. He pulled back, but she followed him, pressing her breasts to his bare chest. She felt so good against him, so damn good in his arms.

He tightened his arms around her and just held her for a moment. But his body heated and the tension built. And just holding her would not be enough.

He had to have her—had to taste her—had to be inside her. He moved his hands to her waist and undid the button of her jeans. The zipper rasped as he lowered it. And his pulse pounded harder from the noise. She'd let him do that, just as she'd let him take off her sweater and bra. But would she let him push down the jeans?

She stepped back before he could reach for them. And his breath caught and trapped in his lungs. She was going to stop him.

He could understand why...

She blamed him for her coming out on the losing end of her divorce and in the media. But, as he'd pointed out, it hadn't hurt her career any, not like she was trying to hurt his by turning in those forged memos to the bar association. Since she'd done that, he should be so damn mad that he shouldn't be attracted to her at all.

And he *was* damn mad, more pissed off than he could remember being in a long time. But even then he couldn't find her repulsive. She was too damn beautiful and sexy to resist. Not that he wanted to resist.

He wanted her too much for that and, more important, he wanted her to want him too much.

But he wouldn't be able to do that if she kept stopping him.

She just stared at him now, her gaze on his bare chest like a caress. He could feel her touch, feel her skin even though a couple of feet separated them now.

Then she took another step back and turned away from him toward the control panel. He held his breath, waiting for her touch a button and get the elevator moving again.

But if she were going to do that, wouldn't she first put her bra back on and her sweater? Instead of reaching for her discarded clothes, though, she pushed down her jeans and revealed a tiny bow on a G-string at the top of her perfect ass.

Ronan fisted his hands at his sides so he wouldn't reach for her. Just because she'd undressed didn't mean she intended to have sex with him. Maybe she only intended to torture him. Maybe—like turning those documents over to the bar—it was her way of getting revenge on him.

Seeing her like this—so bare and beautiful—and not being able to have her, might be worse than losing his law license...

What the hell was she doing? Muriel asked herself the question again, but like before, she couldn't come up with an answer. Sure, she knew what she'd thought she was doing: carrying out the plan she'd concocted to bring Ronan Hall to his knees and get him to tell her the truth.

But nobody brought men like Ronan Hall to their knees. Not women. Not men...

They were too tough. Too powerful.

In their lives and most especially in the bedroom. She'd heard all the stories about him—not just how ruthless he was in court but how ruthless he was in relationships. She'd worked with some of his ex-girlfriends. He was always the one who'd ended things and always too soon for the women concerned.

No matter how ruthless he'd been, the women had wanted more. Some had even admitted begging.

So Muriel was the one who needed to worry about being brought to her knees. Again.

He'd already done it once—in the courtroom. Now she had to worry about him doing it here. Because when he touched her...

When he kissed her...

He made her want him more than she'd ever wanted anyone before. Just like all those other women had told her.

He wasn't kissing or touching her now. She could put her clothes back on and restart the elevator. But when she bent over to pull up her jeans, a strange noise filled the car.

It was raw and guttural, a groan full of pain, as if the man who'd uttered it was being tortured. Ronan was the only other one inside the elevator, so she turned toward him.

He was on his knees now. But even on his knees, his head was above her waist. He was so damn tall and broad.

And so damn sexy.

His breath was hot as it whistled between his clenched teeth and brushed across her abdomen. Her stomach muscles tightened as tension wound inside her, streaking from her nipples down to her core.

"You're perfect," he murmured as his lips brushed across her skin.

She could have snorted and reminded him that that was not what he'd claimed in court. Then she had been anything and everything but perfect.

But she couldn't say anything. She couldn't even move. She was frozen as she waited for him to touch her again.

His lips skimmed softly across her stomach to her hip, then lower over the lace of her panties. And through the thin lace, she could feel his hot breath move over her mound. He touched her with his hands, too. They moved to her ass, cupping it in his palms. And somehow his fingers must have tugged so gently at the bow that she hadn't felt it release. But her panties fell.

And nothing separated his mouth from the essence of her. He flicked his tongue back and forth across her clit as he lifted her, moving her legs over his shoulders. Then he feasted on her—sucking on her before sliding his tongue inside her.

And Muriel melted, heat and pleasure flooding her. He lapped at her—licking and sucking and driving her out of her mind. She whimpered, moaned and arched back. Without the wall of the elevator behind her, she might have fallen. The wood was cold and hard against her back. But she didn't care.

She had the heat and strength of Ronan. She clutched at his head as he continued to move his mouth over her. His tongue flicked and teased. And he raised one of his hands to her breast, sliding his palm over it and the taut nipple.

She cried out as she came, the orgasm shuddering through her with such intensity that tears burned her eyes. And she understood why women begged him for more.

Despite that release, *she* wanted more.

He hadn't pulled back. He continued to lap at her as if he couldn't get enough of the taste of her orgasm. But that wasn't what she wanted now.

She wanted him. She wanted to feel him inside her.

She slid her legs off his shoulders and tried to stand. But her body was too limp from pleasure, her muscles too loose. And her legs folded until she was on her knees in front of him. She'd already opened his shirt, so she pushed that and his suitcoat from his shoulders. Then she reached for his belt.

But he caught her hand.

And she wondered now if he was going to stop her. She froze as she remembered all the times that had happened in her marriage. She wasn't the sex addict that her ex and those witnesses had claimed she was. But she'd certainly needed it more than her husband had.

He'd had an excuse every time. He hadn't felt well. Or he was tired.

But she'd always wondered if it was her fault. If she just wasn't that desirable…

But Ronan's dark eyes burned with desire for her.

His thumb stroked over her wrist, over her leaping pulse. His voice was a rough rasp when he murmured, "If you touch me now, I'm going to come right away. And I want this to last."

So did she.

But just his words—and that gruff, sexy way he'd uttered them—had her on the verge of coming again, especially when his gaze moved over her like a caress.

He licked his lips, which were wet with her orgasm. And he groaned. "You taste so damn sweet. I could go down on you all night."

"We don't have all night," she reminded him. They only had until someone noticed the elevator wasn't moving and got working on the problem. "We have to hurry."

She didn't care if he came quickly. She just needed him to come—inside her. With a condom, of course, though. She always practiced safe sex. She reached for the bag she'd dropped onto the floor. She had to have some inside.

Didn't she?

She didn't need it. Ronan pulled one from his wallet. Then he was standing. He unclasped his belt and unzipped his pants.

Her breath caught and held as she waited for him to push them and his silk boxers down, and when he did, she released that breath on a gasp of shock and awe. He was huge—so long and thick and throbbing...

She wanted to touch him with her hands and with

her mouth. She wanted to suck on him the way he'd sucked on her. But when she reached for him, he caught his fingers in her hair.

"We don't have time," he reminded her. And there was regret in his voice.

He wanted her to go down on him. She could see it on his face as he stared at her kneeling in front of him. She flicked her tongue out to tease him and that same groan of torture he'd uttered before filled the elevator car.

But he stepped out of his pants. And he ripped open the packet and sheathed himself in the latex condom. He must have had them specially ordered because it covered more of him than she imagined any store-bought ones would have.

"You are so big…" she murmured breathlessly as a moment of fear flicked through her. Would he fit?

She couldn't wait to find out. She lay down on the floor of the elevator. And as he watched, she ran her hand down her body—from her throat over her breasts, down her abdomen, to where she was already wet and throbbing. As she moved her fingers over her mound, she moaned and squirmed, so ready for him.

And that groan tore out of him again. "You're going to make me come just looking at you," he warned her. But then he dropped to his knees again.

Instead of moving between her legs, though, he lifted her so she straddled his thighs. Then he lifted her more, and she nearly stood so she could ease herself down onto his cock. She guided him inside her, her inner muscles rippling and grasping at him. Even as wet and ready as she was, she had to stretch and arch to accommodate his girth. She could feel his cock pulsating with the same desire that filled her.

And the tension was on his handsome face, in the beads of perspiration on his brow and the rigidness of his clenched jaw. He lowered his head and kissed her. And as his tongue slid into her mouth, he thrust deeper into her body. His hands caught her hips, and he guided her down, then up.

They moved together in a frantic rhythm as the pressure built inside…

Muriel nearly sobbed with the need for release. She was close to something she instinctively knew would be more powerful than anything she'd felt before.

With just his mouth, he'd given her an overpowering orgasm. With that cock…

That enormous, throbbing cock…

She couldn't imagine the pleasure he could give her. Then she didn't have to imagine, as her muscles began to clench. He reached between them and flicked his thumb over her clit—once, twice…

And she screamed as pleasure gripped her. She came and came…

And came…

Then he was coming, too, his hands gripping her hips tighter and he drove her harder against him. Then he tensed and yelled. And his body shuddered with release.

Shock gripped Muriel now. Instead of being frozen or limp, she was filled with panic. What had she just done?

That scream she'd uttered...

She'd never cried out like that before. But then, she'd never felt anything like that before.

And that scared the hell out of her. So she moved quickly. She jumped up from his lap and rushed around to grab up her clothes. Her hands trembled too much to mess with Bette's bows now, so she just pulled on her jeans and her sweater and shoved the lingerie into her bag.

Ronan dressed, too, but not as quickly as she did. And he glanced around the elevator as he did up the buttons of his shirt. His hands were completely steady.

And she hated him for that along with all the other reasons she'd already hated him. She hated that what they'd just done seemed to have had so little effect on him. But then, he had sex all the time.

She was the one who'd been reduced to using battery-operated partners for her pleasure—because of him. So maybe it was only fitting that he'd given her such pleasure.

He owed her.

But he'd also given her panic. Someone must have heard them, was probably investigating even now. She was going to wait a moment before she restarted the elevator, though. She didn't want someone to see them stepping off it and realize what they'd just done...

The whole damn car smelled like sex—like orgasm and perspiration.

Sweat trickled down between her breasts.

"Is there a security camera in here?" he asked. "Is that what has you so freaked?"

She gasped at the horrible thought. She was afraid they would be caught. She hadn't considered that they might already have been caught on camera.

Why hadn't she considered that there might be security cameras in the elevator? With her luck, there probably was, and then someone would sell the footage and her sex tape would be splashed all over the internet.

Her sex tape with Ronan Hall...

She should have been horrified. Instead, she felt a little flicker of excitement at the thought of being able to watch it herself, to see what he'd done to her. What she wanted him to do again. But if she turned to him now, he would think that everyone had been telling the truth about her—that she was a sex addict.

Her hand shaking, she slapped the button to restart the elevator. She had to find a security guard. She had to make sure that if there was a tape, she got the only copy of it.

"You can't even look at me?" Ronan asked.

And if she didn't know him better, she would have

thought she heard hurt in his voice. But from all those weeks spent in court with him and all those interviews she'd watched that he'd given, she did know him better. She knew he didn't care about other people's feelings because he didn't have any of his own. There was no way she could have hurt him.

No way that she would…unless he lost his law license because of her complaint. She felt a twinge of regret over reporting him to the bar, but then she reminded herself of all those weeks in court, of all the lies that had been told about her, of all the reporters who'd hounded her for interviews.

She shook her head. No. She couldn't look at him now. And it should have been because she was disgusted over what she'd just done and with whom she'd done it. No, she couldn't look at him now with as much as she wanted him again.

Still…

Those orgasms he'd given her had only made her hungry for more. Her plan had backfired. She wasn't going to bring him to his knees, at least not in the way she wanted. But she was very afraid that he would bring her to her knees and she would stay on them, begging him for whatever pleasure he would give her. It was better that she never see Ronan again—except on video if that security tape existed.

She almost hoped that it did.

CHAPTER FIVE

TOO BAD THERE hadn't been a security camera in the elevator. Then Ronan would have been able to watch the tape and verify that he hadn't just dreamed what had happened that night over a week ago. He would have known for certain that he had actually had sex with Muriel Sanz, the most beautiful woman in the world.

He wasn't being romantic or fanciful when he thought that. He was just repeating the fact that the world had already declared. She had recently been voted The Most Beautiful Woman in the World by Celebrity International, and she was on the cover of every magazine and all over the internet. He couldn't get away from her.

And yet he hadn't seen her in several days. Now he wasn't sure that what had happened had actually happened. He hadn't gotten any release from the tension that gripped his body even now.

But maybe he was tense because of this meeting his partners had called. Before anyone at the conference table spoke, he knew what it was about: him.

Tuesday was their usual day to discuss Street

Legal business. This was Friday. Of course, the meeting could have been about their partner Stone Michaelsen's upcoming murder trial. It was the highest profile case he'd had yet—representing a billionaire accused of killing his young bride. What if his case had been compromised? They suspected they had a mole in the office. Some notes from Ronan's partner, Trevor Sinclair's case files had been given to his opposing counsel. Trev still won the trial against the major pharmaceutical company, so it hadn't been a big issue for him.

Not like those *notes* about Ronan that had been turned over to the bar association. Even though those had been forged, they could still affect him. He could lose his license or at least be sanctioned. And if that happened, it could affect the practice, as well.

He glanced around the table at his three partners. These guys were more than business associates. They were friends—longtime friends. If not for them, he wouldn't have survived the time he'd spent on the streets as a teenage runaway. And because they were his friends, he needed to fix this so it didn't affect them at all.

"Don't worry," he told them, because it was clear from their somber gazes and rigid jaws that they were worried. "I've got this handled."

"You know who the mole is?" Simon asked hopefully. As the managing partner, he'd taken it upon himself to find the source of the leaked information, but he'd found love, instead.

Ronan would have preferred, and not just for self-ish reasons, that Simon had found the mole. It would have been less dangerous for his friend than risking his heart.

"No." Ronan shook his head. "I don't know that…" The source had to be someone in their office, some-one who had access to their case files.

"We need to find out," Trevor said. He was still pissed that his big civil trial had nearly been com-promised. Then he added, "You need to find out, so you know who the hell is behind this mess with the bar association."

Warmth flooded Ronan. Trev cared about him. They all did. And he, despite his reputation for car-ing about nothing but winning, cared about them.

"I'm sorry," he said.

"I'm the one who was supposed to find the mole," Simon said.

"And it's not like Muriel Sanz's claims are true," Stone added with unwavering support. "There's no way you would ever suborn perjury."

He was glad that they knew that, that they believed in him. If only Muriel could do the same…

She had to know the truth, or she wouldn't have had to forge the documents. And despite her claims to the contrary, she must have been the one who'd forged them. But if they were credible enough for the bar to investigate, they must have looked authentic. How had she pulled off that without some help?

"Thanks," Ronan said. "Glad you guys know that."

"You don't have to cheat to win," Trevor said.

"Not anymore," Simon murmured. He'd been a con artist, trained by his father at an early age to deceive people. Without Simon's cunning and charm, Ronan and his partners wouldn't have survived the streets. "But someone else is cheating. It was one thing to take notes from our files, but to forge them?"

"Maybe they only took the letterhead," Trevor said, "and that model forged the documents."

That was what Ronan believed—or had believed. After their interlude in the elevator, he wasn't sure what he believed anymore. He wasn't even sure he believed *that* had happened. He was still so damn tense and needy—for her. He hadn't even bothered trying to ease that ache and tension with another woman. He knew only Muriel would satisfy him now—until he'd had enough of her.

Stone snorted derisively. "You think she's smart enough to do that?"

Ronan tensed even more. "She's not some empty-headed bimbo!" he snapped in her defense. It wasn't like his friend to stereotype just because of her job. Ronan had known and dated plenty of smart models and so had Stone. "She's not an idiot."

Stone shook his head. "I looked over your case file. She had to be an idiot to marry *that* guy."

"A lot of intelligent people marry the wrong people," Ronan said. His father had been one of them, and he was a brilliant man in all matters but love.

"I don't doubt that," Stone said. "But you're the one who painted her as the empty-headed bimbo."

"He and Allison McCann," Trevor said with a sigh that sounded almost regretful.

He used Allison McCann's PR firm, McCann Public Relations, in all his trials, too. But then, Trevor handled the high-profile civil cases. Ronan handled the high-profile divorce cases.

Hell, everything Street Legal handled—down to the trusts and wills Simon wrote up—was high profile because of their reputation and their clients.

"It wasn't just me and Allison," he said. "It would have been all those witnesses she claims lied about her, too." Was she telling the truth? He needed to know. He needed to know what the hell was fact and what was fiction.

Like if he'd really had sex in the elevator with The World's Most Beautiful Woman or if he had only dreamed it.

"Bette thinks they did," Simon said.

"Bette is her friend," Ronan reminded him. And that friendship went both ways. Muriel had defended Simon's former assistant, as well.

Simon tensed. "You don't still think Bette had anything to do with Muriel getting that letterhead?"

He couldn't rule it out, not until he had all the

facts. And apparently he wasn't the only one. Both Trevor and Stone glanced at Simon then quickly looked away.

"You all think she could have?" Simon asked.

"They're friends," Trevor said.

"So are all of us," Simon said. But instead of adding on whatever point he'd meant to make, he cursed.

"And we'd all lie for each other," Trevor finished for him.

Simon sighed. "Yeah, we would. But Bette wouldn't lie to me."

Ronan snorted. He'd never known a woman who didn't lie. And he couldn't believe that his streetwise friend had become so naïve.

Yeah, falling in love was a mistake for everyone. It was a mistake that Ronan would never make.

Instead of getting angry, Simon just shook his head, as if he pitied Ronan. Simon was the one who'd tied himself down to one woman. His plan had been to seduce Bette to find out if she was the office mole, but she had wound up seducing him, instead. She'd conned the con.

Simon was the one deserving of pity. Not Ronan.

"Why do you think she won't lie to you?" Ronan asked. And he was honestly curious now.

"Because she loves me."

Ronan snorted again.

"She really loves me. It's not infatuation, not lust—it's real," Simon said.

And Ronan was sad for him, that he believed love was real.

"Too bad you couldn't pull that off," Stone said. "If you could make Muriel Sanz fall for you, you could get her to withdraw her complaint to the bar association."

"They're really taking that seriously?" Ronan asked. Stone had a source at the bar.

His friend grimly nodded.

"Damn it!"

"Try the seduction idea," Trevor suggested. "It worked for Simon."

Simon chuckled. "It worked because I could get close to Bette. Muriel Sanz hates his guts. She's never going to let him close enough to seduce her."

Oh, she had let him close—close enough to kiss her and touch her and taste her and fuck her brains out and his, too.

What if there had been a camera in that elevator?

They hadn't thought about that until it would have been too late. They hadn't thought at all. And Ronan hadn't talked about it. He hadn't told his friends about either time he'd run into Muriel. He'd figured they would get worried that he had only made the situation worse and pissed her off more.

He was kind of worried that he had. She hadn't even been able to look at him after...

Stone sighed. "And Ronan doesn't have your charm, either, Si. You're right. It would never work."

"Want to bet on that?" Ronan asked.

Simon laughed again. "What—are you playing truth or dare right now?"

They'd played that game on the streets, daring each other to take stupid chances or tell the truth about the shitty lives they'd run away to escape. Ronan had always taken the dare. He intended to play that game with Muriel Sanz now.

He dared to try to get the truth out of her. "It's a dirty job," he said, "but someone's got to do it."

"I would make the sacrifice," Stone said with a lustful sigh, "if I wasn't just about to start this killer trial."

"I can do it," Trevor offered, and his blue eyes twinkled with lust. "I'd like to do The World's Most Beautiful Woman."

"No!" The shout surprised Ronan, especially since it had slipped through his own lips—just as some strange emotion coursed through him, tightening his stomach into knots and clenching his hands into fists. Was this jealousy?

It was something he'd never experienced. He had never been possessive of anyone before. Hell, he'd set up his friends with some of his exes in the past. Maybe that was the issue, though. He hadn't had enough of Muriel Sanz yet.

"I know you think she's a hellcat," Trev said. "But I can handle myself. In fact, I kind of like it rough." He chuckled.

And Ronan wanted to slug him. What the hell was wrong with him? These were his friends. He gritted his teeth and shook his head. "I will handle it," he said. "I've already talked to her a couple of times since she turned me in."

Trev leaned across the table and intently studied Ronan's face.

"What?" he asked, unnerved.

"I'm looking for the claw marks."

He touched his cheek.

And Trevor chuckled again. "She hit you."

"I had it coming."

"Oh, I'm sure you did," Trev said. "So what makes you think *you* can handle her?"

He wasn't sure that he could, but he damn well intended to try. "She's my problem," he said. "I've never had a problem I haven't been able to handle."

There was a sudden silence around the table. And they all glanced away from him like they had Simon when he'd been so certain that Bette wasn't lying. They knew there was one problem he hadn't been able to handle, not without running away: his parents.

But he wasn't going to run away this time. He sighed. "Come on, guys, that was a long time ago. I can handle Muriel Sanz." And he intended to put his hands all over her until she screamed again like she had in the elevator.

Or at least that was what he thought she'd done. He had to make sure he hadn't dreamed it all.

"Just remember what you're really after," Simon advised. "You want her to withdraw her complaint to the bar."

"And tell you where she got those documents," Trevor added with a quick glance at Simon.

Before they could start arguing again, Ronan stood up from the conference table. "Challenge accepted," he said, as he headed toward the door. But as he walked away, he realized Muriel Sanz might prove to be the biggest challenge of his life.

The doorbell pealed, making Muriel flinch. It had been ringing nonstop for days, ever since she'd received that ridiculous title that magazines made up to sell more issues. She wasn't certain who even voted on these things. Her—The World's Most Beautiful Woman?

Yeah, right.

The bell sounded again, so she picked her way through her suddenly overcrowded apartment to the door. When she peered through the peephole, all she saw were flowers—a colorful profusion of orange tiger lilies and red gardenias and yellow tulips. They were really beautiful. She couldn't refuse them. With a sigh, she pulled open the door.

"You must be getting tired of bringing all of these up," she said.

But then the flowers moved, revealing the face— the unfairly handsome face—of the man who carried them. It wasn't Howard, the gray-haired doorman with so many wrinkles he looked like a bulldog. This was the man who'd been haunting Muriel's dreams, keeping her awake in her tangled sheets.

He didn't look as though he'd lost any sleep the past week. What a damn good-looking man. He must not have come from the office because he wore jeans and a T-shirt now, which left his arms bare—the muscles bunched up impressively with the load of stuff he carried.

"What are you doing here?" she asked, her pulse quickening as she realized that he had somehow figured out which apartment was hers. Just the way he'd tracked her down at work, he had tracked her down at home.

He held up a bottle of wine that was in the hand not holding the arrangement. "We never went for that drink." His dark eyes gleamed with naughtiness as he must have been remembering, like she was, why they hadn't gone for that drink.

They had quenched their thirst in the elevator instead. No. That had just wetted Muriel's appetite for more...of Ronan Hall.

"You're not here for a drink," she said as his gaze skimmed over her.

She wasn't dressed like The World's Most Beautiful Woman now. She wore an old pair of yoga pants and a tank top. But he stared at her like she was wearing only her Bette's Beguiling Bows lingerie. Maybe he could see beneath the thin tank top and nearly threadbare pants.

He stepped forward, and she instinctively stepped back, which allowed him to pass in front of her and enter her apartment. Along with the wine bottle, he held up a big bag from which spicy and mouthwatering scents wafted. "No, I brought dinner, too. I remember you were hungry that night."

"That was over a week ago," she reminded him. "I've eaten since…" But she *was* hungry. It wasn't for the food in that bag, though. She was hungry for him. Then her stomach growled, and she remembered that she hadn't eaten lately.

He chuckled. "Not today."

She snorted. "Not for a couple hours."

He glanced down her body again. "You don't starve yourself?"

She laughed now. "I wouldn't look like this if I did."

He nodded and a little groan slipped out between his lips. "No. You wouldn't. I'm glad I didn't bother bringing a salad, too."

"What did you bring?" she asked, even as she knew letting him stay would be stupid.

They wouldn't just have wine and food. They'd have sex, too. And maybe that was why she was going to let him stay.

She really, really wanted sex with him again. She wanted to know if it was as good as she'd thought it had been in the elevator. Or maybe it had just seemed like that because it had been so long since she'd had sex with anything but her vibrator.

"I brought Carmine's."

She pointed to the bag. "I can see that."

"Pasta ragù and chicken parm…"

Her stomach growled again. "Good choices. And the wine?"

He held up the bottle again—it was in the same hand with the food. "Pinot noir."

How could he have known all of her favorites? Then she remembered. She'd had to do an interview for the magazine that had bestowed the ridiculous title on her. She narrowed her eyes as she studied his handsome face. "You've done your homework."

He didn't deny it. Just grinned that damned sexy grin of his again. And his dark eyes twinkled. "Lucky for me your favorites are also mine."

She didn't know if she believed that or not. She doubted she could believe much of what he said. But she didn't care at the moment. She was too hungry, and not just for the food.

She took the bag from his hand as she led him toward her small dining area. The table overflowed with flowers, too, like the coffee table and the narrow foyer table. The flowers were the only vibrant color in the apartment she had wanted to be a serene oasis for her after the chaos the divorce had made of her life. The walls and ceiling were white, as was all the furniture. And the floors were bare with no varnish or stain darkening the white oak.

"Looks like a funeral parlor in here," he remarked.

"You're not the only one who read that article," she said. "These are all for congratulations." From people she'd never even met, from designers and photographers and even a few movie producers. She shuddered a little, thinking of all the attention she'd garnered.

He held out the flowers. "Congratulations."

She shrugged. "I had nothing to do with it." If anything, it was probably because of him and all the publicity over the divorce trial. But what she added was, "Just genetics…"

He laughed. "So you're not denying you're beautiful?"

"Should I feign some modesty?" Too many people had told her she was beautiful, starting with her very honest grandparents, for her to say otherwise.

"You'd be lying if you did," he said.

She gave him a pointed look. "And I don't lie."

He didn't argue with her. He just grinned again and held up the bottle of wine. "Screw?" The grin widened and his dark eyes glittered with mischief. "Corkscrew, I mean."

She stepped through an archway into her tiny kitchen and took one from a drawer in the white cabinets and handed it to him. Then she pulled down some plates and grabbed some silverware. This time she did intend to eat and drink first.

But she had no doubt what they were having for dessert: each other.

CHAPTER SIX

WATCHING MURIEL EAT was torture…

She closed her eyes and savored each bite, little moans of pleasure slipping between her lips. After swallowing the food, she would flick her tongue across her lips as if to clean up any drop of sauce or missed morsel. Then she would lift the fork to her mouth and slowly part her lips, beginning the decadent process all over again.

Ronan had never gotten hard watching someone eat before. But he was now, so hard that he couldn't taste the food in his own mouth. He could only chew it and wash it down with a sip of wine.

She was too distracting. Too damn irresistible…

His body was tense, his cock pulsating with the need to be buried inside her. No. He wasn't hungry anymore. After pushing his plate aside, he took another sip of the wine.

Then he murmured, "I'm surprised you let me in."

She glanced up at him as if only just realizing he was still in the room. She'd been so focused on her food that she might have forgotten all about him.

Ronan flinched as his ego took the hit. Nobody forgot his presence—until now.

"You're not the only one," she murmured. "But I was hungry."

"I'm glad I brought food, then."

"Thank you," she said. "You didn't eat much yourself." She gestured at his plate.

"I wasn't hungry…" For food. His stomach was clenched into too many knots for him to eat anything. But her…

He wanted to taste her again like he had in the elevator. Wanted to see if she was as sweet as he'd thought she'd been, as addictive.

Not that he would ever get addicted to anyone. He knew how dangerous that could be, and he was not about to make that mistake—not even for The World's Most Beautiful Woman.

"Why are you here?" she asked him.

Ronan opened his mouth and the truth almost spilled out because he had no problem with telling it how it was. But if he told her what he was up to— seducing her into dropping the complaint with the bar association—she would undoubtedly kick him out of her apartment. So he couldn't tell the truth. At least, not the whole truth.

"I came because I can't stop thinking about the other night in the elevator."

"That was scary," she said.

It had been scary. He couldn't remember ever

wanting anyone the way he'd wanted her. But that had been then. He wanted her even more now, especially after watching her eat. He wanted to watch her do something else.

Him.

"I thought we were going to plummet to our deaths," she added.

Ronan realized what elevator incident she was talking about, and it wasn't the one he'd been thinking about, the one that had never left his mind, keeping him awake and hard every night and pretty much every other waking moment since it had happened.

But had it actually happened?

Or had he wet-dreamed the whole thing?

"It wouldn't have happened if you hadn't kept messing with the control panel," he reminded her.

Her green eyes twinkled as she stared across the table at him. "I like testing control."

Realizing she'd been teasing him, he grinned and asked, "Yours or mine?"

"Both," she replied. "But I failed that test in the elevator."

"Is that why you couldn't look at me afterward?" he asked. That had bothered him. Did he disgust her so much that she had been embarrassed she'd had sex with him? Or had she been embarrassed over where they'd done it?

She sighed. "I can't believe we didn't think about

cameras." She looked at him with suspicion. "Or had you thought about them and just not cared?"

He shook his head. "Honestly, I wasn't thinking at all." Just feeling an overwhelming attraction to The World's Most Beautiful Woman.

Her eyes remained intent as she studied his face, as if trying to determine if he was being honest.

"You're the one who's famous," he said. "Don't you assume there are always cameras on you?"

"I don't know if I'm famous or infamous now," she said. And it was clear that she blamed him for that. "But I should be getting used to cameras always being on me."

There had been some paparazzi staked out in front of her building. But he suspected she was aware of that. It was probably why she was home on a Friday night. Of course, it was early yet. Maybe she intended to go out after dark.

"Yes, you should," he said. "I think you're going to have more than fifteen minutes of fame." He had already discovered she was more than a gorgeous face and perfect body. She was smart and strong, too.

She shrugged off his assurance. "The next scandal will come along, and the media will forget all about me."

He shook his head. "Not a chance."

Still staring at him, she sighed. "Not if I keep hanging out with you," she agreed.

"You think I'm going to embroil you in another scandal?" he asked.

"Just spending time with you is a scandal," she said. "You're the man who represented my ex in court, the man who destroyed me."

He leaned back a little and was able to reach through the dining room archway into the living room. Her place was small, but she'd lost the penthouse in the divorce—thanks to him. He picked up the magazine he'd seen on an end table and held up the cover with her face emblazoned across it. "You don't look destroyed."

With all her recent success, she should be able to afford a bigger place than the one she'd lost.

"I'm resilient," she said.

"Yes, you are." He could relate. He'd survived a lot so far in his life. He could even survive this—whatever this thing was with her.

A dare. The guys had dared him to get her to withdraw the complaint. He could get her to do that. He emptied the wine bottle into her glass.

"Are you trying to get me drunk?" she asked.

"On one bottle of wine?" he asked, and lifting his own glass, added, "One that I'm sharing with you?"

"Maybe you think I'm a lightweight."

Now he studied her face. She had that twinkle in her eyes again. "I bet you could drink me under the table."

"We could have a contest," she suggested.

"Now who's trying to get who drunk?" he asked. He didn't want to be drunk. He had enough trouble maintaining control around her when he was sober. He pushed his glass away from him.

And she made a clucking-chicken noise at him.

He laughed. The woman was one surprise after another, the biggest being that she kept letting him get close to her. Could she feel the same attraction for him that he felt for her?

"I am a little scared," he admitted, and he wasn't just teasing now. "Of you."

She grinned. "You believe your own smear campaign? You really think I'm a man-eater?"

"Yes."

"I am still hungry," she said. But she'd already pushed her food aside. Now she shoved back her chair. Instead of standing up, though, she dropped to her knees and disappeared beneath the table.

Then he felt her hands on his thighs, her palms sliding up them to reach for his zipper. He pushed back his chair now. But he couldn't quite stand, not with his legs beginning to shake slightly.

His cock shook, too, pulsating with the desire coursing through him. "What are you doing?" he asked, his voice gruff.

"Testing control..."

He didn't need to ask whose this time. He knew. His. He was in trouble. Big trouble. But there was no way he could hang onto control with her touching him. Yet he was powerless to stop her. She unclasped his belt and parted the fly of his jeans before pushing down his silk boxers to free his cock. It nearly jumped into her hands. And a giggle slipped through her lips.

"A little eager," she mused.

He'd been wanting this, imagining this, dying for this…the moment when she would close her full lips around his shaft…

She took her time. First she slid her hand up and down the length of him, pumping him into madness. Then she leaned forward and flicked her tongue over the head.

Ronan nearly lost his head, a groan tearing from his throat as he leaned back. He could feel the cords in his neck straining as the muscles in his stomach knotted. Tension wound tightly inside him. Then her tongue slid down the length of him, right to his balls.

He groaned again and murmured, "What are you doing to me?"

Torture, he suspected, and he couldn't deny that he had it coming. He wanted her so badly, wanted her to close her lips around him and take him deep in her mouth so badly that he would give her whatever she wanted from him.

This wasn't the way it was supposed to be, though. He was supposed to be seducing her. Instead, he had been seduced into total compliance.

This was her chance. Muriel knew it. His big, muscular body was nearly trembling with the passion overwhelming him. He was close to losing control.

If she pulled back now…

If she stopped…

She might be able to make him beg for more. And she might be able to trade her sexual favors for the truth. But would she ever be able to believe what he told her?

At the moment, she didn't care about the truth, though. She only cared about the heat and the passion coursing through her. She wanted him. She wanted to taste his cock and his orgasm. She wanted to drive him as out of his mind as he'd driven her in the elevator a week ago.

So she closed her lips around him and sucked. He arched up from the chair and groaned. Then his fingers clutched in her hair, tangling but not pulling. He wasn't pulling her away. He was holding her close.

He needed the release. She could feel the tension in his body. He fairly vibrated with it. And his cock moved in her mouth; she could feel his pulse pounding madly in his engorged flesh. Hers matched the crazy rhythm of his. She was so excited, so stimulated just from giving him pleasure. Her pulse pounded in her clit and her nipples were taut, pushing through the thin lace of bra and the tank top she wore.

She moaned and sucked his cock deeper, to the back of her throat. Then she slid her lips up and down and around, teasing him to madness.

His fingers clutched her hair more tightly. But she felt no pain, only more excitement. Teasing him was teasing her. She had never wanted anyone the way she wanted him. He was so damn gorgeous—so big.

She stroked her hand up and down the rest of the length of his erection.

And finally he came, yelling her name as his big body tensed and shuddered. She drank him the way she had the wine, savoring every drop. His taste was rich and complex—just like the man.

He panted for breath, his head back, his body limp until she eased away. Then he moved quickly, reaching for her. He lifted her up in his arms and swung her around as he checked out the place.

"Is this a studio?" he asked. He must have been looking for the bed.

She pointed to a door. "One bedroom…" It was a small room. The bed nearly filled the entire space, which was good because he got to it quickly and lowered her to the mattress that was covered with fuzzy white pillows and silky white sheets. She'd wanted to feel as if she was sleeping on a cloud when she went to bed.

He stepped back. And she wondered for a fleeting, anxious moment if he was just going to leave her there. After all, he'd had his release, and he was known for being a ruthless man. But never a selfish lover…

Finally he moved, shoving down his jeans and boxers. Then he kicked off his shoes and lifted his shirt over his head. His washboard abs and muscular chest rippled with the action.

And a moan slipped through her lips. "You could be a model," she mused. He was that good-looking.

He laughed as if she'd told him an absurdly funny joke.

But she was serious.

"No, you really could," she insisted.

"I watched your shoot," he reminded her, as if she would ever forget his gaze on her while she'd been photographed in all those different lingerie outfits. "I couldn't sit still that long. I couldn't hold the poses, couldn't handle the heat of all those lights, and most of all, I couldn't follow the photographer's orders."

"No, you couldn't," she agreed. Modeling was much more grueling work than most people realized. She was oddly pleased that he knew and respected how hard it was. Not that she wanted his respect or anything.

Especially after the way he'd treated her in court.

But she did want him. She wanted him inside her, filling her, like he had in the elevator. He was already starting to recover, his dick beginning to swell and rise again as he stared down at her lying on the pillows.

She lifted her hips and wriggled out of her yoga pants, kicking them off to join his clothes on the floor. Then she lifted her tank top over her head and showed off her latest outfit from Bette's Beguiling Bows.

It was green. Bette had designed it to match Muriel's eyes. And she'd given her the first prototype of it as congratulations after that magazine named her The World's Most Beautiful Woman. This bra had the cups laced together with the bow at the top of them. So she had to take her time, untying that bow before pulling the ribbon loose.

"You didn't model that," he said, whistling with appreciation.

"Bette just made it for me to celebrate that magazine title," she said.

"It's better than flowers," he said with a gruff sigh as he stared at her.

She took her time undoing the lacing, stroking her fingers over her cleavage as she pulled the ribbon free. Even before she pulled off the bra, Ronan was completely hard again.

The panties were designed the same way, laced up to a bow on each hip. Before she could even undo the first bow of the panties, Ronan joined her on the bed. He lowered his body onto hers, but he kept most of his weight off her as he braced himself on one elbow. Then he leaned down and covered her mouth with his. He kissed her gently at first, which was such a surprise that she gasped, her breath shuddering wistfully out between her lips.

Then he deepened the kiss, moving his tongue inside her mouth. He teased hers with the tip of it.

She nipped at it with her teeth, gently biting, and

he groaned. Then his hands moved over her, his palms sliding over her shoulders and arms before moving to her breasts. Finally he touched them, and she arched off the mattress, pushing her breasts into his palms. He squeezed gently, massaging the swollen flesh, before focusing on her nipples. He rolled them between his thumbs and forefingers, teasing them to even higher points.

Heat and wetness surged between her legs as her mound swelled and throbbed. She writhed beneath him, needing more, needing him. She was now as desperate as he had been moments before and he had barely touched her yet.

"Ronan…" She murmured his name, not caring how much like a plea it sounded. But she didn't want to be the only desperate one, so she touched him again, stroking her fingers over his chest, down his washboard abs to his shaft. She wrapped her fingers around it.

But he pulled back and moved down her body, his hanging half off the mattress while he pressed kisses to her shoulders and her collarbone and finally her breasts. He closed his lips around one taut nipple and continued to rub the other between his thumb and fingers.

She arched her body up and moaned.

"You are so damn responsive," he said, his voice gruff with his own passion. "You're probably already wet for me."

Instead of fighting with the bows, he just pushed the panties down her legs. And he moved his hand over her mound. His fingers slipped easily inside her, and he groaned. "Very wet…"

Then he shifted farther down her body and made her wetter as he flicked his tongue over her clit. He teased her to madness. She clutched the bed and then his hair and screamed his name as the tension broke with a shattering orgasm.

Her body shuddered.

She clawed at his shoulders and his back, trying to drag him up her body. "I need you," she said. "I need you inside me." She didn't care that she sounded exactly as she'd been portrayed—like a sex addict—a man-eater. He was the only man she wanted to eat at the moment.

He groaned again. But then he pulled away.

And she nearly screamed in frustration…until she heard foil tear. Then he was back on top of her, pushing inside. He was so big. She lifted her legs. And he pushed them higher, over his shoulders. Fortunately, Muriel was flexible. She pushed her legs against her breasts, teasing her already sensitive nipples. Ronan pumped hard—thrusting in and out of her. But Muriel matched his rhythm, arching up and pushing against him.

She was so close…

So close to release, but before she could find it, he pulled out. Then he was rolling her over, moving her around as easily as if she was a doll. Despite being a model, Muriel was no lightweight. Her ex hadn't even been able to carry her over the threshold on their honeymoon. Ronan would have no such problem. Not that he would ever carry her over a threshold.

But he lifted her easily and positioned her with her back to him, her bottom up, and he found her again, sliding inside her. His hand moved over her mound, teasing her clit. He reached farther up her body and teased the nipples of her swaying breasts. And he drove his cock deep inside her.

Muriel rocked her hips back against him, meeting his thrusts as the tension built unbearably. As he touched her and thrust, she shattered as an orgasm overwhelmed her. She shuddered as her muscles clenched before relaxing; she was satiated with pleasure.

Ronan drove deep once more before tensing and uttering a deep groan. His hand on her breast squeezed, exciting her all over again. Despite the powerful orgasm he'd just given her, she could have gone again. And again and again…

Was she addicted to sex—with Ronan Hall?

CHAPTER SEVEN

RONAN'S HANDS WERE SHAKING. Hell, his whole body was shaking. But he forced his fingers to clench into a fist, and he pounded on the door. There was a bell. He could have used it, but he suspected his hand was shaking too much for his finger to find the small button.

He'd had no problem finding every one of Muriel's buttons. And he'd pushed them. Just like she'd pushed his. They'd driven each other wild. Maybe that was why he was here.

He was crazy. He had to have been crazy to leave The World's Most Beautiful Woman lying naked in her bed. But he'd had the feeling—that urge that he'd had when he was a kid and he'd been overwhelmed with his parents' fighting—the feeling that compelled him to flee.

So he'd fled.

He hadn't gone far, though, just a few floors up to another apartment in the same building. He lifted his hand to knock again just as the door finally opened. He was taken aback for a moment by the face that stared at him. While it was familiar, it wasn't the one he'd expected to see, although he should have known Simon would be with Bette Monroe if she was home. He suspected his friend spent every free moment with his former assistant. Simon's shirt was off and his blond hair was mussed, so it wasn't difficult to imagine what they'd been doing.

The same thing he'd been doing with Muriel...

Simon looked more shocked to see him, his blue eyes narrow and his brow furrowed with confusion. "What the hell are you doing here? Did you get lost?"

Despite feeling a little lost—the way he had when he'd run away all those years ago—Ronan shook his head.

Just as Simon had back then, he took Ronan in. He opened the door to Bette's apartment and led the way down a short hall to a good-sized living room. The apartment was bigger than Muriel's and nicer, with highly polished hardwood floors and dark trim. Maybe designers actually earned more than models.

Or maybe Muriel hadn't been able to afford anything bigger after paying out the divorce settlement Ronan had gotten for her ex...

He flinched as guilt stabbed him. Of course that didn't matter anymore. With all her recent accolades, she had to be back on top now.

On top...

Why the hell hadn't he tried that position with her? But then she would have been able to set the pace and drive him even more out of his mind than she already had. When she'd gone down on him, he'd nearly lost consciousness, the pleasure overwhelming him.

Simon turned back toward him and asked, "What are you doing here? I thought you were going to try to seduce the truth out of Muriel tonight."

"What?" Bette exclaimed as she walked up behind her boyfriend. She was pulling the belt tight on a silk robe that was probably all she wore. "That's horrible!"

Ronan wasn't about to remind her that was what Simon had done with her. He had already caused enough trouble between them.

But apparently Bette hadn't forgotten because she slapped Simon's shoulder and said, "It was bad enough when you tried that with me."

"It was bad?" he asked, as he turned toward her and arched one of his blond brows.

She uttered a wistful sigh, and her mouth curved into a naughty smile. "Very bad…"

Simon stepped closer to his girlfriend and wound his arm around her small waist, drawing her against his side. His hand smoothed over her hip, and his gaze dipped toward where the neck of her robe began to gape over her full breasts.

Ronan snapped his fingers. "Hey, I'm still here!" He didn't mind being part of a threesome—if the other two were women. That was the only way he didn't mind sharing. But somehow he didn't think that would be the case with Muriel. He wouldn't like sharing her with anyone.

But if her reputation was to be believed, she wasn't seeing only him. There had been all those flowers in her apartment, too, and only people she knew would have known where to send them. According to her ex, one man had never been enough to satisfy her. Of course, that one man hadn't been Ronan.

He could satisfy her. At least, he thought he had.

"Why are *you* here?" Bette asked him. She obviously wasn't very happy to see him, not that he could blame her. He hadn't been very nice to her at her going-away office party.

He wondered if she would ever forgive him. And if she couldn't, Muriel certainly never would. But what was there to forgive?

He had only been doing his job. Ronan was not the one who'd done anything wrong. Muriel was. Wasn't she?

"I came here to ask you about Muriel," he replied.

"Bette already told you she had nothing to do with those documents that were given to the bar association," Simon said. And now his voice was as cold and unwelcoming as his girlfriend's.

"Muriel said those documents were given to her," Ronan said.

And she was the one who'd given them to the bar association. But why? If she had really done what those witnesses had said, why would she have been so upset? And why would she seem so certain that those witnesses had lied?

His blood chilled with the thought that they might have committed perjury. But no. He couldn't be wrong.

"And I don't know who gave them to her," Bette said. "Muriel doesn't even know."

"How well do you know her?" Ronan asked.

Bette glared at him now, and there was a defensive snap in her voice when she replied, "Very well."

He didn't want to piss her off, especially not with Simon present. But he had to ask, "How do you even know her at all?"

"What do you mean?" Simon shot that question at him, and his voice was sharp, too, in defense of his girlfriend. "What are you getting at, Ro?"

Ronan sighed with frustration. "I just don't understand their friendship."

Bette obviously understood what he was getting at because she answered Simon. "He doesn't understand how we can be friends because Muriel's beautiful and famous, and I'm not." Hurt flashed in her dark eyes.

And Ronan flinched. That wasn't what he'd really meant, but it was a valid reason for them not to be friends. They seemed to have very little in common.

Simon's arm tightened around his girlfriend's small waist. "You're beautiful and famous, too, sweetheart."

She laughed, but with no bitterness or resentment. "Not like Muriel." But she didn't appear to be jealous of her friend. "She's The World's Most Beautiful Woman."

Ronan agreed with her, but Simon apparently didn't. Before he could argue with her, Ronan interjected, "That's not what I meant at all. Bette, you're sweet and nice and honest…" At least, he hoped, for his friend's sake and his, that she was. "And Muriel Sanz is not."

Bette laughed again. "Yes, she is. And that's why we're friends. I have never met anyone more straightforward or honest than Muriel is."

He shook his head. It wasn't possible. "But…that's not what all those witnesses said."

"They lied," Bette said as if it was just that simple.

His doubts escaped in a snort of derision. "Really? All of them?"

"Why is it so easy for you to believe that Muriel is the one who lied?" Bette asked. "Because she's a woman? Because she's beautiful?"

Ronan narrowed his eyes now. How much did Bette know about his life? About his past? He turned toward his friend.

Simon shrugged. "She's intuitive."

"And a good judge of character," Bette added. "I trust Muriel. I believe she's telling the truth."

Ronan didn't want to believe it. Because if she was telling the truth, then she had every reason to hate him. Hell, he would hate himself.

He shook his head, refusing to accept it. All of

those people wouldn't have lied. No. Muriel was the liar and the manipulator, perhaps better even than his mother had been. He had to be careful. He had to protect himself before he got in too deep.

But he had a sick feeling that it might already be too late for that. He'd been smart to leave her alone in bed tonight and run. He probably should have run farther than he had, though, because he would have a hard time stepping back into that elevator and not pressing the button for her floor, not going back for more of her.

For the first time in his life, Ronan was beginning to understand his father. He was beginning to understand how a woman could become an addiction.

What would it take to cure him?

Losing his license?

Would that finally kill his attraction to her?

The doorbell rang, and even though she'd been waiting for it, the sound startled her. And Muriel realized she'd dozed off on the couch. She opened her eyes and squinted against the sun streaming through the tall windows.

After what they'd done in the bedroom, she wouldn't have been able to sleep there, not on the tangled sheets that had smelled of Ronan and sex. She wouldn't have been able to sleep there because she would have just lain awake, wanting more. But she must have been the only one who'd wanted more, because Ronan had taken off in a hurry.

Had he been late for a date with another woman?

Not that their dinner together had been a date. He hadn't asked Muriel out; he'd just shown up with take-out. And, embarrassingly enough, she had been home alone on a Friday night. But it had been a Friday night, so of course, he'd had plans. No wonder he'd left in such a hurry.

But she'd been certain he would come back, that he had been as affected by the attraction between them as she was. But he hadn't returned.

Unless that was him at the door, persistently ringing the bell. Maybe he'd brought her breakfast.

Her stomach rumbling at the thought of food, Muriel rolled off the couch and hurried down the short hall to the door. When she pulled it open and found her friend standing in the hall, disappointment flashed through her.

Feeling guilty, she pushed it aside and gave Bette a bright smile. The pretty brunette held a beverage carrier and a bag that was already getting soggy from whatever greasy bounty she'd brought with her. Muriel stepped back, but her friend remained standing in the hall.

"Is *he* here?" she asked.

Muriel tensed. She hadn't told Bette that she'd run into Ronan—a couple of times—lately. No doubt Bette would think she was a fool for even talking to him, let alone letting him get as close as he'd been to her.

Inside her…

She shivered despite the fact that she'd pulled on her yoga pants and a sweatshirt after he left. "Is who here?" she asked, stalling for time.

Could Bette think she'd been hooking up with someone else? Maybe some magazine had printed some more lies about her. But Bette knew better than to believe what she read about Muriel.

"Ronan Hall," Bette said.

The heat of embarrassment rushed to Muriel's face.

"He's playing you," her friend warned. "He's trying to seduce you into dropping your complaint with the bar association."

A pang struck Muriel's heart. Not that she was hurt or anything…

She'd suspected Ronan was up to something, that he'd had a reason for seeking her out in the elevator and at her photo shoot.

She plucked a cup of coffee from the beverage carrier Bette held in one hand. "At least let me have some caffeine before we start this conversation."

She was exhausted. Not just because of the marathon sex she'd had with Ronan but because she hadn't been able to sleep after he'd left.

She'd wanted him again. Hell, she wanted him now.

Bette held up the grease-stained bag. "I brought doughnuts, too."

"I love you," Muriel said as she ushered Bette into the apartment and closed the door behind her.

"You love too easily," Bette said.

Feeling like her friend had struck her, Muriel gasped. "I am not in love with Ronan."

"I should hope not," Bette said.

"I hate his guts," Muriel reminded her.

"Then why are you even talking to him, let alone sleeping with him?" Bette asked.

Muriel silently cursed him for being a tool and herself for being a fool. She should have known that he would brag to his friends, and Bette was seeing one of those friends. Simon Kramer wasn't much better than Ronan. All of the partners of the Street Legal law practice were notorious for being ruthless lawyers and lovers.

"I could say the same about you and Simon," Muriel reminded her.

"You could have in the beginning," Bette admitted. "But I am in love with him now. And he loves me."

She didn't doubt Bette's feelings for her former boss, and he actually seemed invested in the relationship, too. He certainly spent enough time at her place.

"That's not going to happen with me and Ronan," Muriel said. He'd skipped out right after they'd had sex.

"I know," Bette agreed. "So what the hell are you doing with him?"

"We're not *sleeping* together," Muriel murmured as she thought of everything they'd done to each other, everything she wanted to do with him still. "I'm playing him, too."

Bette's brown eyes darkened with obvious skepticism. "How's that?"

"I want to get him to admit the truth," Muriel replied. "I want to make him confess that he coerced all those people to lie about me on the witness stand."

Bette glanced away from her then. Did she not believe that those people had lied?

"Do you think they were telling the truth about me?" Muriel asked.

"No," Bette quickly replied. "Absolutely not. But I'm not sure that Ronan got them to lie about you." She dumped out the doughnuts onto the table.

Muriel reached for a powdered one. She knew it would be custard filled; those were their favorites. Before she took a bite, she asked, "Then why would they?"

Bette shrugged. "Why does anyone do anything?"

"For money," Muriel replied. "Or fame."

"Exactly," Bette said.

The people who'd testified against her had gotten both. The interviews they'd given after the trial had brought them their fifteen minutes of fame, and the magazines and television networks had probably paid for those interviews.

Could Ronan really have not suborned perjury?

"But what about those memos?" Muriel asked.

Bette sighed. "I think they were forged."

"You believe Ronan?"

"He's too smart to put anything incriminating in writing," Bette pointed out.

And she was right. Ronan was smart. If he'd done something illegal, he wouldn't have risked someone discovering what he'd done. He probably wouldn't have documented it. Were the memos she'd received forged, as he'd claimed?

She cursed. She wouldn't have filed her complaint with the bar association if she hadn't been certain they were authentic. "But why would someone have given them to me?"

Bette sighed. "Someone is making trouble for Street Legal," she said. "They've given case file notes to opposing counsel for another trial…"

"But were those notes real?" Muriel asked.

Bette nodded. "But that doesn't mean the ones you were given are," she said. "I really don't think Ronan would have been so careless." Her throat moved as she swallowed, as if she was choking on her words, before she added, "And I don't think he would have suborned perjury."

"Not even to win?" Muriel asked. Ronan Hall was all about winning. He had freely admitted that in every interview he'd ever given.

"He doesn't take cases he doesn't think he can

win," Bette replied. "So maybe he's telling the truth, too."

But Muriel couldn't be certain that was the case. And until she was certain, she wouldn't withdraw her complaint from the bar association, no matter how many times Ronan seduced her. Yet if getting her to withdraw her complaint was what he wanted, why hadn't he asked her to do it?

He hadn't asked her anything during or after sex. He'd dressed quickly and hightailed it out of her bedroom and apartment as if he'd been late for something else.

Or someone else…

Now she felt a curious pang of emotion, one that left a bitter taste in her mouth despite the sweetness of the custard and powdered sugar. It couldn't be jealousy; it must have just been disgust. Anger surged through her.

"Even if he didn't know those people were lying, he treated me like trash," Muriel said. "He dragged my name through the mud. I will never forgive him for that."

"Good," Bette said. "I don't want you to fall for the wrong man again and get hurt."

"I won't," Muriel assured her friend. But she had a sick feeling in the pit of her stomach, and it wasn't the doughnut. She'd barely nibbled on that. It was fear.

No. She wouldn't fall for Ronan. It didn't matter

how good the sex was between them. He wasn't a good man. But he was the best lover she'd ever had…

Maybe she would just have to have a lot of sex with him, so much that she would get sick of it, that she would get sick of him.

CHAPTER EIGHT

SUNSHINE POURED THROUGH the wall of windows in Ronan's office. Street Legal's offices encompassed the entire top floor of a building in Midtown. The space was like a loft with high ceilings open to the rafters, exposed ductwork, brick exterior walls and rough-sawn hardwood floors.

Ronan stood at his desk. He had the kind that he could raise, so he could forgo a chair. He didn't like sitting. It was hard enough staying in his seat in a courtroom, which he managed to do only as long as he had to, when the opposing counsel had the floor.

He flipped through the file on his desk, reading over the court transcripts he'd printed out, and he snorted in derision at his opposing counsel in this case. The defendant's attorney had posed no challenge for Ronan at all.

She hadn't raised any of the arguments that Ronan would have, had he been Muriel's attorney. But he hadn't been. He'd been working for her ex.

He remembered Stone's comment at the meeting. The reason Ronan's partner had questioned Muriel's intelligence wasn't because she was a model but because of the man she'd married. Stone didn't have a very high opinion of Ronan's former client, and as Ronan reread his real case notes—not the forged ones Muriel had given to the bar association—his opinion of Arte Armand sank, as well.

Why the hell had he represented this schmuck?

Oh, yeah, he'd felt sorry for the guy. Arte had been a broken man when he'd come into Ronan's office. He'd sobbed out his misery over how horribly his new bride had mistreated him. *New* bride...

They hadn't been married very long at all. Less than a year. The prenup she'd had him sign should have held up—would have held up—had she not been proven at fault in the divorce. Had Ronan not proven her at fault.

Had she been at fault? All those witnesses had claimed she was, that she had treated Arte as horribly as he'd said she had. But if that was true, why had he stayed with her?

Because he hadn't been able to leave, just like Ronan's father hadn't been able to leave his mother? That was why Ronan had taken the case, because Arte had reminded him of his father. But his father had loved his mother for years before she'd started cheating on him. They'd had a child together. He'd had reasons to stay.

What had Arte's reasons been? Money? Or love?

He'd claimed he'd loved Muriel. But if that were true, why had he wanted to hurt her so badly? To publicly humiliate her? And why had Ronan helped him do it?

That twinge of discomfort and regret he'd been having turned into a gnawing ache in his chest now. Had he been wrong? No. That wasn't possible. Not with all those witnesses claiming how badly Muriel had treated her ex…

But as he read their testimony in the transcripts, he noticed how similar their stories were, which had previously convinced him of their veracity. Now he wondered…were they too similar, almost as if every one of them had been reading from the same script?

He felt a shiver of unease chasing down his spine. It wasn't because of the transcripts but because someone stood in the doorway of his office. He turned toward where Muriel leaned against the jamb, watching him.

How had she gotten past Miguel, their receptionist-slash-bouncer? Then he remembered that it was Sunday. Miguel didn't come in on Sundays. Nobody did but Ronan and his partners. Stone had come in, too, to prepare for his upcoming murder trial. And Trev was working on something, as well. Only Simon hadn't come in—probably because he was still in bed with Bette.

Ronan wished he was still in bed with Muriel. He shouldn't have left her Friday night. Right now—as he stared at her, looking so gorgeous in artfully ripped jeans and a sweater with shoulder cutouts—

he didn't know how he'd left her at all when she'd been lying there naked in the sheets tangled from their sexual romp.

Remembering how she'd looked—her silky skin flushed from their passion—his body tensed, and his cock hardened. He wanted her again. Still...

She was so damn sexy and looked almost posed against that doorjamb, the way she had posed for that photo shoot. Then she moved, her hips rolling as she walked slowly toward him.

His hand shook slightly as he closed the file—her case file. He didn't want her to see what he'd been reading. He didn't want her to know that she was getting to him, giving him doubts.

He had to clear the desire from his throat to ask, "What are you doing here?" But the question came out brusquely, his voice still gruff.

"It's good to see you, too," she remarked sarcastically.

It was better than good to see her. Despite her face being everywhere, he'd missed her, and that unsettled Ronan. It wasn't like him to miss anyone but his friends. And he and Muriel were not friends.

They were enemies. Weren't they? She'd turned him into the bar association, and he had...

What had he done?

And what was she doing? She stopped next to his desk and glanced down at the surface of it.

He flipped over her file. "I'm working."

"I'm sorry." She held up her palms, but he didn't mistake it for a gesture of surrender, especially when she added, "I didn't mean to interrupt you ruining someone else's life."

"I'm not," he said. At least, he hoped he wasn't. "And I didn't ruin yours."

"Yeah, right..." She snorted.

"You're on the cover of every magazine and all over the news," he said.

She shuddered.

"Isn't that what you wanted?" Why would she have become a model unless she'd wanted to become famous?

"I didn't want it like this, because of a scandal," she said. "I wanted to know I earned it."

"You did." She had been the most beautiful woman in the world even before the scandal.

She snorted again. "I have been half expecting you or that sleazy PR firm to send me a bill."

He wouldn't put it past that PR firm: Allison McCann was nearly as mercenary as Ronan's mother and maybe Muriel's ex had been. If anyone sent her a bill, though, it would probably be Arte Armand...

"I'm not giving you a bill," Ronan assured her.

He couldn't and wouldn't speak for Allison McCann, though, and he wondered now if he should have let her speak for Street Legal, at least for this case. Had Arte and his friends, who were probably now Muriel's former friends, been telling the truth?

"I don't want your money," he said. He just wanted her—like she'd been the other night, naked and wild for him. His fingers twitched now with the urge to reach for her, to touch her.

"I know," she said. She tossed something down on his desk, right on top of that case file.

"What's this?" he asked as he glanced at the big orange envelope.

"This is what you seduced me for," she said.

He groaned. He should have known Bette would tell her about his plan. They were friends. Apparently better friends than he and Simon were, since Simon hadn't kept that dare a secret for him.

"Muriel—" Before he could say anything else, and he wasn't certain what he could have said, she put her fingers across his lips.

"Don't worry," she said. "I was seducing you, too."

Instead of being offended or furious, he was amused and moved his lips against her fingers as he grinned. He'd wondered why she'd let him close to her. Obviously, she'd been after something, too.

She shivered and pulled her hand from his mouth.

And he asked, "What did you want from me?"

What had she wanted from him? At the moment, she couldn't remember. Hell, she wasn't sure she even knew her own name anymore. All she knew was how he made her feel wanton.

She wanted him so damn badly.

"Right now," she murmured, "I don't know."

"I think you do," he said, and he stepped out from behind his tall desk—which put him right in front of her—so close that his thighs touched hers.

She wore heels today, very high stilettos. Since she was already tall, the heels brought her nearly to his height. But he was ridiculously tall and broad and muscular and handsome.

"It's really a waste that you're a lawyer," she murmured. With his devastating good looks, he should have been a male model. He would have been far more successful than her ex had been.

Ronan must have mistaken her comment for an insult, though, because he flinched. "Everybody hates lawyers."

Not everybody.

"Only divorce lawyers," she teased. "I don't have any problem with your partners."

He narrowed his dark eyes and studied her face with obvious skepticism. "Not even Simon?"

"Not now," she said. "But if he hurts Bette, I'll kill him." She'd never had a friend like Bette—she knew that now, after all those people had given false testimony against her. They hadn't been true friends.

Ronan chuckled and reached for her arm, gently squeezing her biceps. She flexed for him. "I think you could take him," he said. "Hell, you could probably take me."

"I wanted to kill you for a long time," she admitted.

And he flinched again. Then he slid his fingers up to her shoulder and, stroking her bare skin, he asked, "And now?"

Now she just wanted him. She shivered in reaction to his touch. But it wasn't enough. She wanted his hands everywhere on her. She wanted his mouth everywhere.

His name slipped through her lips on a soft, lustful sigh. "Ronan…"

He pressed his mouth to hers. His kiss was gentle at first, just a whisper-soft brush of his lips across hers.

Her breath sighed out in a gasp of pleasure. She hadn't known he could be so tender. It was almost as if he cared about her. But that wasn't true.

She had to remind herself of that—of the fact that Ronan Hall didn't care about anyone or anything but winning. And he wouldn't stop until he'd won, until he seduced her into doing what he wanted. While he wanted to find out where she'd gotten the memos, he also wanted her to withdraw her complaint to the bar association. Bette had warned her.

If she was smart, she would stay far away from him. But she was the one who'd sought him out today. Bette had refused to give her his home address, but she'd reluctantly admitted that he could be at the office, that the partners often worked weekends.

Was that why Ronan hadn't come back to her

apartment? Because he'd been too busy working? Too busy ruining other people's lives to seduce her again?

Taking advantage of her parted lips, he deepened the kiss, sliding his tongue inside her mouth. He stroked his tongue across hers, teasing her, tasting her.

Desire rushed through Muriel, heating her skin and making her pulse race wildly. She didn't care about anything right now—about his motives or hers. All she wanted was the pleasure she knew he could give her.

He pulled back and panted for breath, his eyes dark and wild with desire. "Damn you…" he murmured.

Instead of being offended, she laughed because she knew he felt it, too—the overwhelming attraction between them.

His lips curved into a slight, reluctant grin. "You are becoming an addiction."

Apparently he didn't understand the definition of addiction—because if he was addicted to her, he wouldn't have been able to walk away from her like he had the other night. He wouldn't have been able to leave her bed at all.

There was no bed in his office. She wasn't even sure he had a chair. He'd been standing at that odd desk of his. But she didn't care where they had sex; she just had to have sex with him.

Now.

She understood what an addiction was, and she

was very afraid that she was becoming addicted to him. Her body ached with desire—with need—for his.

She clutched the nape of his neck as she pulled down his head so she could kiss him back. She skipped the tenderness he'd shown her at first, and she went straight for the passion, kissing him deeply and hungrily. She nibbled at his lips and teased his tongue with the tip of hers.

He groaned and lifted her, the muscles in his arms bulging and rippling as he carried her.

She wasn't certain where he was taking her, and she didn't care as long as he took her.

He settled her onto something that was hard and cold beneath her bottom. And when she glanced down she saw she was on the bar that ran along one wall of his office. The surface was black granite with a vein of gold running through it. The faucet on the little sink was gold, as were the liquor decanters sitting next to her ass on the countertop.

"Need a drink?" she asked.

"I need you," he said. And he dragged her sweater up and over her head. Her hair tangled around her face, blinding her for a moment. So she didn't see his reaction to her bustier. It was black leather and, of course, a bow topped the laced-up front of it. But she heard his reaction in the sharp intake of his breath.

Then he groaned her name. His fingers shook slightly as he fumbled with the button of her jeans.

He got it loose, though, and tugged down her zipper, as well. She wore leather panties to go with the bustier. They were also laced up the front and tied with a bow.

"Remind me to compliment Bette on her brilliant designs," he murmured as he lowered his head and kissed her again.

She nipped his bottom lip between her teeth. She wanted more than his kisses. She wanted his dick. So she reached for it, sliding her hand over the fly of his jeans. His cock strained the already worn denim. She jerked his button loose and pulled down his zipper to free him from his boxers.

Then she wrapped her hand around him, stroking her palm up and down the length of his cock. "I need you now!" she said. "I need to feel you inside me."

He groaned. But he didn't protest. In fact, his control must have snapped because he pulled off her jeans and nearly tore off the bow holding up her panties. The leather dropped away from her. But she was still hot, still burning up for his touch. His fingers slid inside her, and he groaned again. "You're so wet."

So ready for him…

She tugged free the bow on the bustier, and her breasts sprang over the tops of the leather cups. The nipples were already tightened and pointing up toward Ronan. He took one in his mouth and swirled his tongue around it.

She moaned and squirmed against his hand. He

moved his fingers inside her while grinding his palm against her mound. Then he flicked his thumb back and forth over her clit. She tensed but then he closed his teeth gently over her nipple and she came, the orgasm shuddering through her.

"Ronan…" She nearly sobbed his name. She tightened her grasp around his cock and stroked harder.

He shuddered and lifted her again. Despite his strength, he stumbled back. Or maybe he'd intended to walk backward, because he dropped into a chair with her astride his lap. He pulled out a condom packet, tore it open and sheathed himself.

Desperate to feel him filling her, Muriel rose up on her knees and guided him inside her. He was so big, so thick, that he stretched her. She arched and took him as deep as she could. He moved his hips and thrust a little deeper.

She'd never been this full, this complete. A moan tore from her throat as passion overwhelmed her. He was so damn good. And as he continued to move his hips, he touched her breasts, teasing her nipples into even tauter points. She bit her bottom lip, but she couldn't hold back another moan.

He drove her crazy. And she wanted to drive him just as crazy. She touched him back, teasing his flat male nipples until they pebbled. Then she reached beneath her butt and stroked his thighs and balls.

He groaned, and the muscles in his neck corded and stood out. "Muriel…" He growled her name like a warning. And sweat beaded on his upper lip and brow as he struggled for control.

She wanted him to lose it, wanted him as wild as he made her. She leaned forward and kissed him deeply before sliding her lips over his granite jaw to his neck. She nibbled on those corded tendons, then suckled.

He clutched his fingers in her hair, tangling it even more than it had already been. He pulled her face from his neck and kissed her, and as he drove his tongue between her lips, he drove his cock deeper into her.

She rocked her hips against him, arching and straining to ease the pressure that had built inside her again. The tension was nearly unbearable. Despite the release he'd already given her, she needed another.

She needed more of the intense pleasure she feared only he could give her. She'd never had orgasms as long or as powerful as the ones he'd given her. Then he stroked his thumb over her clit once more and she came again, screaming his name.

Her name echoed his, as his big body tensed, then shuddered with his own release. Like her, it seemed as though he came and came. As she collapsed against his heaving chest, he wrapped his arms around her. And their hearts pounded in the same frantic rhythm.

Muriel had never felt so close—such a connection— to another human being. But that wasn't possible, not with Ronan Hall. He didn't let anyone close.

And after how she'd been betrayed, neither should she. Remembering how badly she'd been hurt, how badly Ronan had hurt her, she scrambled off his lap. Then she ran back to the bar where he'd taken off her clothes.

"I could use a drink, too," he murmured, as if that was what he thought she needed.

Instead of reaching for one of those decanters, she grabbed up her clothes and donned them in such haste that she didn't realize her sweater was inside out, until Ronan tugged on the tag. Then he reached over her and lifted one of those decanters, and as he did, she noticed his hand was shaking.

Maybe he was as unnerved as she was. He must have dressed quickly, too, because his jeans were up and zipped again. Once he poured the drink, he walked back toward his desk—leaving the route to the door unobstructed.

Instinct prompted Muriel to run for it. If she was smart, she would. But if she was smart, she wouldn't have come here today—she wouldn't have risked seeing Ronan ever again.

CHAPTER NINE

"THIS ISN'T WHAT I seduced you for," Ronan said as he picked up the envelope. After that mind-blowing sex, he wasn't sure he'd seduced her for any reason but pleasure. He had never had as much in his life before he started having sex with her. "It's just an envelope."

With nothing but her name scrawled across the front of it. He didn't recognize the handwriting, not that it was very easy to read since the thick black marker with which it had been written had smeared and bled through the orange paper.

"That's what those documents were in," she said. "Someone shoved it under my door. When I found it, I thought Bette must have slipped them to me."

"It wasn't Bette." He accepted that now. She cared too much about Simon to put their practice at risk.

"No. I don't know who it was," she said with a sigh. "So I guess I haven't given you what you seduced me for."

"I seduced you so you'd go to the bar association and confess that those documents were forged," he explained.

She laughed. "If I agreed to that, you'd be suborning perjury all over again."

"I didn't," he said. He'd never had to coerce anyone into lying. They usually did it freely, on their own. But in this case, he hadn't been aware of anyone lying but her. "I would never do that."

He would never risk his license or the reputation of the practice. He'd worked so hard to get off those streets and help his partners form Street Legal. It meant too much to him. Hell, it and his friends were all he really had.

Muriel's beautiful green eyes were intense as she studied his face, as if she was trying to discern if he was lying or telling the truth. "You freely admit that winning is everything to you."

"In interviews?" he asked. "Press releases? We didn't hire that PR firm to make us look like losers. Who's going to hire an attorney who's okay with losing?"

"Apparently not my ex," she murmured.

"You hurt him badly," Ronan said. He needed to remind himself of that, of how dangerous she was. She'd broken Arte Armand. He had to make sure she didn't break him, too.

She shook her head, and her thick, black lashes fluttered as if she was fighting back tears. "I. Did. Not. Hurt. *Him!*"

Borrowing Simon's gesture, he arched a brow to express his skepticism.

"I didn't," she insisted. "He hurt me."

She wasn't broken, not like Arte had been. She wasn't sobbing. But her eyes were bright. He couldn't be certain those were tears glistening in them, though. He couldn't be certain that she was really feeling anything at all.

Was she still playing him? She'd already admitted that she had been.

"Why did you seduce me?" he asked. Not that he minded. He had quite enjoyed her seducing him. In fact, if he'd enjoyed it any more, he probably wouldn't have survived.

She was an incredible lover. But more than that, they fit, as if their bodies were meant to be together. And their sexual appetites were the same—voracious.

He wanted her again. Even after just having one of the most intense orgasms of his life, he wanted her again. Hell, he needed her.

She stared at him blankly, maybe because of the abrupt way he'd changed the conversation.

So he reminded her, "You said you were seducing me, too. Why? What do you want from me?"

Hopefully more of what they'd just done—a whole lot more—because he wasn't sure he was ever going to get enough of Muriel Sanz.

Her beautiful green eyes narrowed as she glared at him. "I wanted to seduce you into admitting that you coerced those people into lying about me."

He shook his head. "I'm sorry I can't give you what you want, either."

Her full lips curved into a small, sad smile and she murmured, "Then I guess we both lose this time."

He didn't feel like he'd lost until she turned to walk out the door. He couldn't let her leave, not like this. He reached out and caught her, wrapping his hand around her wrist to spin her back to him, back into his arms. Her breasts slammed against his chest, and the breath left his lungs. And as he stared down at her beautiful face, his heart began to pound fast and hard and erratically.

She felt so right in his arms, as if it was where she belonged. But that wasn't possible. Nobody belonged in Ronan's arms. He wasn't the type who stayed to snuggle after sex. And he didn't want to snuggle now.

That wasn't why his arms tightened around her, why he pulled her even closer. He wanted more sex. That was all he wanted...

But there was a strange sensation in his chest, as if it was swelling and warming, and he didn't like the feeling. He didn't like feeling at all. Anything.

Lust. That was all this was, all it could be. Just attraction and lust...

Despite the warmth of his body pressed so tightly against hers, Muriel shivered. The look on his handsome face, with his clenched jaw, was so tense, so almost frightened, that it frightened her, as well.

"What's wrong?" she asked, her voice soft and quavering with the fear she felt in him.

He shook his head. "It should be wrong," he murmured. "But it feels so right…"

"What?"

"This," he said, and he slid his hand from her back down to her hip. Then he rubbed the erection that was once more straining the fly of his jeans against her belly. "Us."

"It is wrong," she said. But she couldn't deny that it felt right between them. There had never been an awkward moment, never any hesitation, never anything but passion. So much passion…

He shook his head again, as if he couldn't accept it.

But he had to; she had to make him—and herself—see that this was wrong. "What would the bar association say if they learned you were trying to coerce me to withdraw my complaint against you?"

He tensed and a breath escaped his lips, as if she'd punched him. "Would you go to them and say that?"

She could. She'd once been so angry with him that she would have. But the passion between them, and the orgasms he'd given her, had eased some of her anger.

"I wasn't trying to coerce you to lie to them," he said. "I wouldn't do that…"

And she was beginning to believe him.

"But you admitted that you want me to withdraw my complaint," she reminded him.

"Yes, but I want you to withdraw it because you believe those memos were forged," he said, "because you believe me." And his dark eyes implored her to do just that.

She closed her eyes. She wanted to believe him. But she couldn't. He'd pretty much told his friends that he was just playing her. So she couldn't believe anything he said.

She shook her head now.

"Muriel…" His breath whispered across her earlobe as he lowered his head and nuzzled her neck. "Believe me."

"I—I can't," she stammered, "any more than you can believe me."

He groaned now and shifted against her again. "I don't know what to believe anymore."

She could understand that. "You don't want to believe me," she said. "Because then you'll have to admit you were wrong."

His brow furrowed. But he didn't deny what she'd claimed. Instead, he lowered his head and brushed his mouth across hers in another of those soft kisses. If she hadn't experienced it, she wouldn't have thought him capable of such tenderness. But just as softly as he kissed her, his fingers slid down her cheek with a light caress.

"What are you doing?" she asked, her voice raspy as she struggled to breathe with the passion overwhelming her. "You have no reason to seduce me

now. I'm not going to the bar association for you."
No matter how much pleasure he gave her.

But he must not have heard her because he continued to please her. His lips slid down her cheek to her neck, and he nuzzled it again, his breath hot against her skin.

She shivered as sensations raised through her. Then his lips were on her exposed shoulder. And she shivered again, but it was heat racing through her—straight to her core. Her nipples tightened, and a moan slipped through her lips.

His mouth moved to hers again, but the gentleness was gone. He kissed her deeply, hungrily. When he pulled away, she panted for breath.

Excitement filled her, making her skin tingle and her pulse pound like mad. Madness was what this was—this obsession that Ronan was becoming for her. It was a madness.

She'd lost her mind.

And her breath…

And her ability to think or move…

It was as if his touch paralyzed her. Her body was going so limp that she might have collapsed if he hadn't lifted her up. This time he didn't carry her far; he just put her on the edge of his tall desk.

He stripped off her clothes until she sat naked on his desk, atop whatever file he'd been reading when she'd walked into his office. So intent on whatever he was reading, he hadn't even noticed her standing there.

But now he'd forgotten all about it. He was totally focused on her. He kissed and touched every inch of her skin, every part of her body.

His mouth moved to her mound, his tongue flicking across her clit. She arched off the desk and cried out as the pressure wound tightly inside her. She needed release, needed him. And suddenly the paralysis was over.

She reached for him, tugging at his clothes—tearing them off—until he was as naked as she was. With her on the tall desk, she was the perfect height for him.

She locked her legs around his waist, pulling him closer until he was as close as he could be. His body covered hers, and she was barely able to tell where she ended and he began. They moved together in a rhythm that was theirs alone, like their song.

It swelled to a crescendo, and they both shouted as they came. Her body shuddered and went limp again on the desk.

And his body began to shake, as if he was as overwhelmed as she was. He stared down at her, and she saw the fear again in his dark eyes.

He had been as overwhelmed as she was.

And she *was* overwhelmed. He made her feel so many things, pleasure most of all. No wonder she couldn't get enough of him. No one else had ever given her such powerful orgasms, such strong releases.

He had a reputation for being an amazing lover. That was why his exes were so upset when he dumped them—because he left them wanting more.

Muriel understood that now. Because even though he'd just given her so much pleasure, she wanted so much more.

And now fear coursed through her. She scrambled down from the desk, knocking off that file as she did. She bent over to pick it up—but he was already there, grabbing up the papers and shoving them back into the manila folder.

So she reached for her clothes, instead. As she dressed, she watched him. He hadn't dressed. He was naked and gorgeous and she wanted him all over again.

This obsession was dangerous, so dangerous that she was tempted to do what he wanted. She was tempted to go to the bar association and withdraw her complaint—even if she'd had every reason to file it.

And she had.

She couldn't forget what he'd done to her in that courtroom and in the media. What he must have done...

No matter how much he denied it, he had to have encouraged those witnesses to perjure themselves. Or maybe she was just like him. She didn't want to believe he might be telling the truth because then she would have to admit she had been wrong—about him, about people she'd once thought were her friends.

About everything...

Like maybe what she was beginning to feel for Ronan wasn't just sex. Maybe there was something more between them than just attraction. Too scared to stay, she headed for the door the moment she was fully dressed again.

This time he didn't stop her. He was too focused on that file again, as if he'd forgotten all about her.

That was what she needed to do: forget all about Ronan. They had no future. And because of their past, they never should have been together. She shouldn't have let him touch her. Now she was worried that his touch was the only one she would want. She should have stuck with the vibrator. She didn't have to worry about her mechanical lover betraying her like every other lover had.

Ronan had betrayed her even before he'd become her lover. She would never be able to trust him.

CHAPTER TEN

THE FIRST TIME he'd met with this man Ronan had felt pity. The guy had been so broken, so upset that his new bride had played him for a fool. And Ronan had been determined to avenge the man, like he'd wanted to avenge his father for all the pain he'd suffered.

But Arte Armand and Muriel hadn't been married very long. How much could he have actually suffered?

Ronan hadn't known her very long, either, though, and he was suffering. His body was tense and aching for hers. And it had only been a couple of days since she'd come here and given him that envelope with her name smeared across the front of it. Had someone given her the memos in that envelope? Or had something else been in it and she was just claiming that it had held those forged memos?

He didn't know what to believe anymore. That was why he'd asked Arte Armand to come to the office. They sat back by the bar where Ronan had had sex with the man's ex. Arte sat across from him, his legs crossed. Ronan could almost smell Muriel—in the office.

A twinge of guilt struck him.

But Arte didn't look as broken as he had the day of their first appointment. His eyes were dry and bright now. His face was tanned, his body relaxed. He wore jeans that were as artfully ripped up as Muriel's had been and a bright pink silk shirt with the cuffs rolled back to reveal the black and white polka dots on the other side of the fabric.

"I'm glad you called," the man said. "I was going to set up an appointment to talk to you, anyway."

"You were?" Had the guy gotten married again? Only a little over six months had passed since his divorce had been granted. That was enough time to get into a serious relationship. But to get married again...

Why would he risk it if his marriage to Muriel had been as terrible as he'd claimed?

"Yes, but I've been busy with the musical I've been producing."

With Muriel's money. And Ronan felt another twinge of guilt—this time for her.

"Really?" Ronan asked. "I didn't know you were interested in theater."

Arte laughed. "Oh, goodness, yes, that's why I moved to the city. I'm a triple threat. I can sing and dance and act."

How good an actor was he? So good that he'd fooled Ronan?

"But you were modeling."

Arte grinned, revealing perfect blindingly white

teeth. "It was easier to break into modeling than acting. But I've found exactly the right vehicle now to launch my career."

Muriel. She had been the vehicle. And Ronan had given him the keys.

"I can't help you with entertainment law," Ronan said. "I'm strictly a divorce lawyer."

"Oh, that's not why I wanted to see you again," Arte replied. "It's about this whole The World's Most Beautiful Woman thing."

Muriel. She was not a thing. Ronan clenched his jaw to hold back his remarks.

"That's because of us," Arte continued. "So shouldn't we get a part of it?"

"I don't want the title," Ronan said. But he was beginning to wonder about Arte Armand.

His hair was expertly styled, the tresses highlighted in gold. The same color that was Simon's natural hue.

Arte laughed again, and it was nearly as high-pitched as a giggle. "Of course not."

"Then what do you want?" Ronan asked.

"Money," Arte replied, as if it should have been obvious.

And it should have been—from their first meeting—that that was what he was all about. Money.

"I think she should give me a percentage of what she's making now," Arte said, "since we made her so famous."

We. Ronan flinched, and his stomach pitched with queasiness from guilt. He wanted to shout at the man to stop saying that—stop giving him so damn much credit for what they'd done to Muriel.

"You weren't married long enough to be awarded alimony," Ronan reminded him.

"But you got me a great settlement."

"Yes, I did." Far more than what Ronan now realized the man had deserved. "And you agreed to that settlement, so you can't go after any more."

"But Muriel would still only be a face and a body with no one knowing her name if it hadn't been for us," Arte persisted. "That should get us something, some percentage of her earnings."

It wasn't Ronan or the PR firm that Muriel should have worried would send her a bill. It was her damn ex.

"It got me a complaint to the bar association," Ronan said. "That's why I called you."

"Complaint?" Arte asked, and he tensed now.

"Yes, Muriel claims I suborned perjury," he said. "She thinks I coerced all those witnesses to lie."

Arte laughed again, but this time it sounded hollow with nerves. "Don't worry about it. She can't prove anything."

"There's nothing to prove, right?" Ronan asked. "I believed those people were all speaking the truth."

"They were—of course they were."

"The same truth, nearly line for line," Ronan

murmured. "As if they'd rehearsed it…" Why hadn't he noticed that before? Why hadn't he questioned them—and Arte Armand—more?

Maybe it was what they'd said about her cheating, about her orgies, that had distracted him from reality and plunged him into the fantasy of a naked Muriel Sanz, insatiable for sex.

Arte shrugged his thin shoulders. "They all saw the same things," he said. "So, of course, they're going to describe them the exact same way."

Now Ronan knew who'd written the script.

"If they were lying, I could lose my license," he said.

Arte reached out and squeezed his arm. "Don't worry. You had no idea."

"That they were lying?" He needed to know. But if Arte admitted to what he'd done, Ronan would probably be tempted to tear him apart. Even now, his hands were clenching into fists.

"No, no, of course not," Arte stammered. "I don't know why she's so upset, anyway. It's not like the trial hurt her or her career…"

That was the argument that Ronan kept giving her, too. But he heard how self-serving it sounded now. "She is upset," Ronan said. And he was beginning to understand why.

Arte uttered a regretful sigh. "Because of her grandparents…"

"What?"

"They raised her after her mom flaked out and ran off," Arte said. "They're real sweet, real conservative people. They must have been devastated."

Over what had come out of the trial, over what Ronan, using McCann Public Relations, had put out there for them to see and hear. He flinched.

Arte sighed again but straightened in his chair. "But they know her, so it's not like they believed..." He pressed his hand to his mouth, as if trying to push the words back in.

"It's not like they believed the lies?" Ronan prodded him.

Arte shook his head. "No, no, not the lies. The truth," he stammered some more. "They wouldn't believe the truth about her. They would only see the best in her."

"That she's straightforward and honest," Ronan said.

And Arte turned toward him, his brow furrowed. "You believe that about her?"

"That's what one of her true friends has said about her," Ronan replied.

"Too bad she hadn't had that person testify," Arte said.

Too bad...

Her representation had been bad. But, ultimately, she'd agreed to the settlement once Ronan had had the prenup tossed out. So she was stuck with it now.

At least she wasn't stuck with Arte Armand any longer.

The slighter man stood. "I wouldn't worry about her complaint," Arte said. "You're a good lawyer."

Ronan had believed that until now. Now he wasn't certain how good he was.

"I'm sure you can get out of it," Arte said. "Are you sure you can't get anything more—"

"No!" Ronan snapped as he jumped up from his chair. He wanted to slug the guy so badly, but he held his fists at his sides. "I think she's lost enough already."

Her money and her reputation. And maybe the respect of the grandparents she loved.

Ronan understood now why she was so angry. And he didn't blame her. He was lucky all she'd done was turn him into the bar association. If he'd been in her place, he might have done far worse—like he wanted to do now to Arte Armand.

A knock sounded at his office door before it was pushed open and a blond head appeared around it. "Hey, oh, sorry to interrupt," Simon said. "We were waiting for you to start the meeting. I didn't realize you were with a client."

"We're finished," Ronan said. For now...

He wasn't entirely sure that he was done with Arte Armand, though. Not after what the man had done—and had made Ronan do—to Muriel.

The guy eagerly walked toward the door, as if

anxious to escape Ronan. Maybe he'd sensed how close he'd come to getting the crap beat out of him. Or maybe he was just anxious to get a closer look at Simon, because it was obvious he was checking out Ronan's partner.

How the hell had Ronan missed that?

How had Muriel? She couldn't have known or she wouldn't have married the man.

As Arte headed toward the elevator, Ronan walked into Simon's office and dropped heavily into one of the chairs around the conference table.

"What's wrong with you?" Trev asked.

Ronan closed his eyes and shook his head. He couldn't even talk about what he had just learned, how big a fool he had been.

"Arte Armand just left his office," Simon answered for him.

"And you realized the guy's a sleaze?" Stone asked with a shudder of disgust.

"Do you know the guy?" Ronan asked, since his partner had made comments before. What worried him about that was that Stone was a criminal lawyer.

Stone shook his head. "I met him in the elevator a couple of times when you were representing him."

"So you didn't represent him?" Ronan asked.

Stone shook his head again. "He's a sleaze but as far as I know, not a criminal."

"He's a con," Simon said from where he sat at the head of the table. "The guy's a con artist."

Ronan sucked in a breath at the managing partner speaking his worst fear aloud. "Are you sure?" he asked.

"Takes one to know one," Simon said. He had been a con artist himself. If he hadn't, they all wouldn't have survived the streets. His cons had kept them alive and fed.

Ronan sighed.

"What does this mean?" Trevor asked.

"I think I could be in real trouble," Ronan said. "Those witnesses lied. If the bar association finds out, they might not believe that I didn't know, that I didn't suborn perjury."

"So you might lose your license," Stone murmured.

Losing his license was the least of his concerns at the moment. He was afraid he'd lost more than that, like his chance of ever being with Muriel again.

Her body tense, Muriel followed the man as he led her down a long corridor. She was stiff and achy. Maybe she should have used her vibrator before this meeting. But she doubted that it would relieve her tension anymore. She was beginning to worry that only Ronan could do that.

And that was why she was here.

"I'm surprised you would want to hire McCann Public Relations," the man murmured over his shoulder, his voice pitched low.

Obviously, he knew Muriel and what his company and Ronan had done to her. Because of that, she wasn't here to hire them. Hell, she didn't need them. Not since she'd been labeled The World's Most Beautiful Woman.

No. What Muriel needed was answers.

She hadn't gotten any from Ronan. So she hoped she could get them here. From Allison McCann. The man stopped at the end of the hall and pushed open a door to a corner office. Sunshine poured through the two walls of windows and glowed like a spotlight on the woman behind the desk.

Allison McCann, with her deep red hair, silky white skin and bright blue eyes, deserved the label of The World's Most Beautiful Woman far more than Muriel felt she did. But Allison McCann always remained in the background.

Muriel wasn't sure how she managed that until the woman spoke, her voice so cool it bordered on frigid. "Ms. Sanz, please come in and have a seat." She gestured toward the chairs in front of her glass desk. "Edward, close the door on your way out."

As the man turned to do his employer's bidding, Muriel caught the look that crossed his face. And she shivered. His boss's voice wasn't the only cold thing in this office.

The door snapped shut with a sharp click, and Muriel jumped. She hesitated a moment before walking toward that desk and that woman.

"I'm sorry..." the woman murmured.

"I didn't come here for an apology," Muriel said. She wouldn't have expected this woman to offer one any more than she expected Ronan to do so.

"I meant for Edward..." Allison gestured at the closed door. "So, if you didn't come here for an apology, why are you here, Ms. Sanz? Are you in need of our services?" She sounded politely hopeful—not pushy.

All the PR people Muriel had met were pushy. She was almost pleasantly surprised, until she remembered what this woman had done to her.

"Why?" Muriel asked. That was what she wanted to know the most.

The woman's lips curved into a slight smile. "That is a fair question, given that you are already extremely high profile right now. But, of course, that is the best time to hire McCann Public Relations, so that we can help guide your career in the direction in which you'd like to go. Please have a seat and tell me where that might be."

Muriel hadn't realized she was still standing. But she was too tense, too anxious, to sit. She walked toward the windows, instead, and stared down at Midtown. Allison had a view of a park from her corner office.

"Do you want to cross over into acting?" Allison asked.

"No," Muriel replied. "I'm no actor." She was too

honest for that. Arte was the one who'd wanted to act and dance and sing.

"Singer?" Allison asked.

Muriel laughed. "God, no." She held up a hand. "And before you ask, I'm not a dancer, either." She had no rhythm—except with Ronan. With him, she always found the perfect rhythm—their movements coordinated to drive each other out of their minds and to ecstasy.

"So you're happy with your modeling career?"

Muriel turned back to study Allison's face. Did she detect some condescension? Some judgment? "Yes, I'm happy being a model."

"Why?" Allison asked.

That was the question Muriel wanted the publicist to answer. But she answered Allison McCann first. "I admire the creativity of the designers. I enjoy show-ing off their hard work." Especially Bette's. She knew how long and how hard Bette had worked to achieve her recent success.

Allison tilted her head and studied Muriel, as if trying to gauge if she spoke the truth. "I could use that quote to get you a lot more work," Allison said. "Designers would love hearing that."

Muriel laughed. "You're always working the an-gles, huh?"

"Is that a problem?"

"It is when you smear innocent people."

Allison jumped up from her chair now. "If you

made this appointment in order to attack me, then you should leave right now."

"If I'd wanted to attack you," Muriel said, "I wouldn't have made an appointment. I would have done it someplace public and embarrassing, like your favorite restaurant or on the street outside. I would have wanted to embarrass you like you embarrassed me."

Allison's pale skin flushed, but it wasn't with embarrassment. It was anger. "I was just doing my job, Ms. Sanz," she said defensively. "You should not be taking this personally or making it personal."

"It was personal to me," Muriel said, flinching as she remembered having to warn her grandparents. Well, she'd tried. But she'd been too late. The story had already broken before she'd had the chance.

Allison shook her head. "Is that why you filed a complaint with the bar association against Ronan Hall? Out of spite?"

Muriel snorted. "Spite? I am not a child."

"You're acting like one," Allison accused her. "Lashing out…"

She was tempted to show this bitch exactly what acting out looked like, but she held her temper. Physically. Verbally she let the other woman have it. "I could sue you for defamation of character," she threatened. "Those witnesses were lying. I have proof of it."

"Forged memos," Allison said with a disdainful sniff.

"That's what Ronan claims," Muriel said. And she was beginning to believe him. "So you've talked to him."

"I work closely with all of the partners of Street Legal," Allison said.

How closely? And did she just work with them? Or was it more than work?

"I know," Muriel said. "That's why I'm here. I want to know whose idea it was to publicly smear me. Yours or Ronan's?" She wanted to cross her fingers in the hope that Allison would take the responsibility. That she would say that Ronan fought her over every press release.

But Allison said nothing. She just sat back down and shook her head.

"I deserve the truth," Muriel said. "Not that I expect you to recognize it."

Allison leaned back in her chair, and her beautiful face twisted into a tight grimace, like she'd sucked on a particularly sour lemon. "You wasted your time coming here," she said. "Unless slinging your insults will make you feel better…since all your recent success obviously hasn't."

"So you're of the same school of thought as Ronan," Muriel said. "That the end justifies the means."

Allison just tilted her head and studied Muriel through those icy blue eyes of hers.

"It doesn't," Muriel told her. "Not when the means

were so mean…" Tears stung her eyes now, and she rushed toward the door. When she opened it, she slammed into the body standing outside it.

And she nearly plowed over Allison McCann's assistant who'd obviously been listening at the door. "If I'd known why you were here," he whispered as he led her through the reception area toward the elevators, "I could have told you that you were wasting your time."

"I should have known I wouldn't get any answers here," Muriel agreed as she blinked back her tears of frustration.

It was Ronan's fault that she was so damn frustrated. She wanted him so badly. But she didn't want him if he was really the man she'd originally thought he was—the liar, the ruthless lawyer.

Who was he?

"You should have asked me," Edward said as he led her toward the elevator.

Muriel stopped. "You know?"

"I sit in on all of Allison's meetings," he said, "except for this one."

Apparently he was the one to whom Muriel should have spoken. Maybe that was why Allison hadn't allowed him to sit in.

The elevator dinged and the doors slid open to the empty car. Before she stepped inside, Muriel turned to him and asked, "So whose idea was it to smear me?"

"Ronan Hall," the man replied.

And Muriel felt as though she'd been punched in the stomach.

"Allison really felt horrible about it," Edward continued. "But she has to honor her client's wishes."

"And Street Legal is her client," Muriel said. Not her.

She'd just been a hapless victim.

"It was Hall's idea," Edward continued. "He's the worst one of those bastards from Street Legal."

"Are they a pretty big client for McCann PR?" she asked.

"The biggest," Edward said with a regretful sigh. "And the most ruthless."

So Allison McCann would probably not help Muriel out with the bar association—even if she knew for certain that Ronan had suborned perjury. And Muriel didn't know for certain. She'd begun to believe him.

But now she wondered if she'd been played—exactly the way he'd bragged to his partners that he would play her into withdrawing her complaint.

Edward continued, "That's why she had to do what Hall wanted. I'm sorry for what happened to you."

Before stepping into the elevator, she squeezed his arm in gratitude. His apology was nice, but it wasn't the one she wanted.

The person who owed her the apology was Ronan.

CHAPTER ELEVEN

RONAN NEVER SAW it coming. Muriel's apartment door barely opened before two hands planted on his chest and shoved him back.

"You son of a bitch!" Muriel yelled at him.

"I guess I had that coming…" he murmured. But she didn't even know about his mother—about how big a bitch the woman had been.

"Yes, you did!" Muriel said, her voice shaking with anger. Then her green eyes widened with surprise as she stared at him. "You admit that you do?"

What did she know? That he'd talked to Arte? He wouldn't put it past the little bastard to have approached her and directly asked for money. No. He probably wouldn't be that direct. He'd be sneaky and underhanded. Like Simon had said, Arte was a con artist.

"What exactly are we talking about?" he asked.

She pushed him again. But she wasn't strong enough to hold him back. He stepped inside the apartment and kicked the door closed behind them.

"What?" she asked. "Are you afraid that someone might overhear us? Are you afraid of making a scene?"

He laughed. "I don't care what people think."

"Yeah, right," she scoffed. "You don't want the bar association thinking you did anything wrong."

"I didn't," he said.

But he was beginning to believe that he had. Even if it was unknowingly.

"I talked to Allison McCann," she said.

"That bitch!" Outrage coursed through him. "She gave you a bill?"

Muriel laughed. "No. She thought I was going to hire her, though." And she laughed again until a snort slipped out. Then she tensed.

And he laughed.

"She is a bitch," Muriel said. "But she's a bitch who's loyal to Street Legal. She wouldn't tell me who ordered the smear campaign."

His stomach churned with the guilt swirling through it. "I did."

"I know," she said. "Edward told me."

"Who's Edward?"

"The bitch's bitch."

He laughed as he realized she was referring to Allison's assistant.

"Why did you do that?" she asked. "Why did you have to smear me in the press, too?" Hurt darkened her green eyes. "Wasn't it enough to beat me in court? You won. Why did you have to win that badly?"

Tears streamed from her eyes, but she squeezed them shut. Then she turned away from him as if she was embarrassed that she was crying.

He wanted to reach for her, to comfort her. Her tears were killing him. But he knew he couldn't take back what was already done. He owed her something, though.

Maybe it was because she turned away that he was able to tell her the truth. Not about talking to Arte.

He wasn't ready yet to admit how wrong he'd been. But he could explain why he'd been wrong.

"I did it for my dad," he said.

She turned back then, her brow furrowed in obvious confusion. "What? That makes no sense…"

"I take every divorce case for my dad," he said. "Because he should have divorced my mom. But he could never bring himself to do it—no matter how badly she treated him, how many times she cheated on him."

"Ronan…" She touched him, just her fingers on his arm.

But his skin tingled with the contact and he shivered in reaction. Or maybe he was just suddenly very cold as he relived some of those moments from his past.

"They fought all the time," he said.

"That must have been horrible," she remarked, her voice soft with sympathy.

He wasn't looking for sympathy. He just wanted

her to understand. "It was…so bad that I ran away. That's how I met Simon and Stone and Trevor."

"On the streets…"

She must have heard the story. Allison McCann had put out several press releases touting the rags-to-riches story of the lawyers of Street Legal.

"So all the stories about you and your partners were true?" she asked.

He nodded. "Yeah."

"It must have been rough."

He chuckled, but with a bitterness he'd never been able to leave entirely behind him. "Living on the streets was safer and easier than living at home."

"Are your parents still together?"

He shrugged. "I don't know. My father and I don't talk about it anymore." But they talked once a week—about the weather, sports, the practice…anything but his parents' marriage. That was the arrangement he'd made with his father—once he'd contacted him again. "And I want nothing to do with my mother."

"I am not your mother," Muriel said. "I didn't cheat on Arte."

"I know that now," he said. "I'm sorry."

But he knew an apology was not enough to make up for what he'd done to her. He wasn't sure what it would take for her to forgive him. Moreover, he wasn't sure what it would take for him to forgive himself.

* * *

Muriel watched Ronan turn away from her and head for the door. He was just going to walk away?

"Coward!" she called after him.

He stopped and glanced back at her over one of his broad shoulders. "What?"

"You're running away again, just like you did when you were a teenager," she said.

His lips curved into a slight grin and amusement glinted in his dark eyes. "You think I'm running from you?"

"Maybe…"

Or he was running away from what he'd done.

Or from what he'd admitted to her about his past.

"I didn't think you wanted me to stay," he said.

"I shouldn't have lost my temper like that," she said.

"You're a passionate woman." His dark eyes gleamed with passion of his own.

And Muriel's heart began to pound fast and furiously. Even as angry as she was with him, she had missed him. Badly. Her body ached with an emptiness only he had been able to fill.

He stepped closer to her. "You're the most passionate woman I've ever known."

"Is that a nice way of calling me a slut again?" she asked as she tried desperately to hang on to her anger. It was safer to be mad *at* Ronan than to be mad *about* him.

He chuckled. "I never called you a slut."

"Liar."

"I just let other people call you that," he said, and his handsome face twisted into a grimace of regret. "I'm sorry about that."

"You believe me now?" she asked.

He opened his mouth, but the words didn't come. He wasn't any more sure of her than she was of him.

But did it matter right now?

She wanted him too much to care about the past. Neither of them could change that. It had already happened.

She wasn't worried about it happening again. She wasn't married now. She probably wouldn't get married again. Obviously, she couldn't trust her judgment.

And because she couldn't trust her judgment, she wasn't ever going to risk her heart again. So she was safe having sex with Ronan—because sex was all it would ever be.

She also wanted a little revenge, though, for all the terrible things he'd had McCann Public Relations spread around about her.

"Muriel," he began.

But she pressed her fingers to his lips to stop him. "Shh…" she said. "Don't say anything you don't one hundred percent believe."

He closed his mouth.

And regret tugged at her. But after what he'd told

her about his mother, she shouldn't have been surprised that he would find it hard to believe her—especially when so many people, people she'd thought were her friends—had testified against her.

He touched her chin, tipping it up. She hadn't even realized she'd bowed her head.

"I'm sorry," he murmured again.

She shrugged. "I don't believe you one hundred percent, either."

After Arte and those people she'd thought were her friends had betrayed her, she couldn't trust anyone, least of all the divorce lawyer who'd represented her ex.

He flinched but said, "I understand."

"But tonight, it doesn't matter what's truth or fiction," she said. "Tonight, nothing matters but pleasure…"

"I'll give you pleasure," he promised as he lowered his head and brushed his mouth across hers. His lips clung, nibbled, and his breath panted out between them.

It had been too long since he'd kissed her. It had only been days but it felt like years. Long years.

And she knew in this he spoke the truth. He would give her pleasure. But that wasn't all she wanted tonight. She stepped back, away from his kiss.

He opened his eyes and stared down at her, his jaw tense, as if he was worried she had changed her mind. So she reached for his hand and tugged him along with her toward her open bedroom door.

And he chuckled. "So you're going to take me up on my offer?"

She wouldn't have been able to refuse. "I have one of my own," she told him as she dropped her hand and walked over to her closet. "Let me show you a really good time."

"Did Bette design something new for you?" he asked, and he almost sounded like a kid asking if Santa Claus had delivered presents.

"Bette's always designing something new," Muriel said—with surprise that her friend could think of so many things to do with bows. "I guess she's been particularly inspired lately." Thanks to his friend.

"Lucky for me," he murmured.

"Not tonight," she said. "Lingerie isn't what I have in mind." She pulled out the sashes of a couple of bathrobes and grabbed a couple of scarves. "This is what I had in mind…"

His dark eyes narrowed, and his grin slid slightly away from his handsome face. "What do you want to do with those?"

"Tie you up, of course…"

He laughed, but it wasn't with amusement now. "And what? Take pictures of me lying there naked and helpless to sell to some tabloid? Or will you just leave me here?"

If he was naked and helpless, she doubted she would be able to leave him.

She shook her head. "I want to tie you up so that you can't touch me. Only I can touch you. Only I can please you."

He stepped closer to her and pulled the makeshift bindings from her hand. "This is about control," he said. "And you know it."

Heat rushed to her face as she remembered how smart he was. Of course he would know that she wanted to be in control and she wanted to take his.

That was going to be her revenge for what he'd done to her—to drive him out of his mind. But maybe she didn't need to tie him up in order to do that.

He'd driven her out of her mind every time they'd had sex, and he had never once restrained her.

But she tugged on the ties he held now and murmured, "Ronan, please…" as she stared up at him through fluttering lashes.

He chuckled and murmured back, "No…" He bunched the ties into a ball, which he threw out into the hallway. Then he kicked the door closed, as if he didn't trust her not to try to use them on him.

"You really don't want me to tie you up," she said.

"I really want to touch you," he told her. And then he proceeded to do just that as he reached for her shirt and lifted it over her head. After he tossed it aside, her hair swirled back down around her bare shoulders.

She had skipped the bra entirely tonight. "Sorry—no Bette's Beguiling Bows..."

His hands were already cupping her breasts. "I don't mind. If I'd known you were braless..."

"What?" she asked.

He leaned down and brushed his lips across one nipple. Then he replied, "I would have done this sooner." And he licked the other one.

She shivered as pleasure coursed through her. She wanted him so badly.

"Aren't you glad you didn't tie me up?" he asked as he moved his hands to the waistband of her yoga pants. After pushing down the knit material, he stroked his fingers over her bare ass. She'd skipped the underwear, too, tonight. "I can give you much more pleasure when I can touch you."

But when he touched her she lost control—and she was losing it now.

Her legs trembled, her pulse raced. She was one more lick or stroke away from an orgasm already. That was how quickly and powerfully he affected her.

And she wanted to do the same to him.

So she reached for him. He must have come to her right from work or court because he wore a suit and tie again. She loosened the tie first and pulled it free from the collar of his crisp white shirt. As she pulled the expensive blue silk through her hands, she stared up at him.

"Don't get any ideas," he warned her, but there was

a chuckle in his voice and a glint in his dark eyes. He pulled the tie from her hands and tossed it aside. He definitely did not trust her yet.

So she went to work on his buttons, revealing all the sexy, hair-dusted muscles of his impressive chest. Then she pushed the shirt and his dark gray jacket from his broad shoulders and reached for his belt. He pulled that from her hands, too, though, and undid his own button and zipper before kicking off his pants, boxers and shoes.

Then he was as gloriously naked as she was. And she went wild for him, touching and kissing him everywhere. She stroked her hands over his ass and down his hard thighs as she dropped to her knees in front of him. Then she closed her lips around his cock and sucked him deep into her throat.

He groaned. And she could feel him shaking.

She hadn't needed to tie him up. She could make him lose control without any ropes or bindings.

But he didn't lose it entirely. He pulled her away before she could make him come. Then he lifted and tossed her down onto her bed. She bounced slightly up from the mattress and met his chest as his body covered hers.

They were a tangle of arms and legs, but their mouths met and mated, kissing each other deeply. His tongue stroked over hers as his fingers slid inside her. He moved his fingers in and out of her until she arched up and whimpered at the orgasm shuddering through her.

But it was nothing compared to the pleasure she knew he could give her. He pulled back—only to don a condom—and then the head of his cock eased inside her. He lifted her legs to his shoulders, so he sank even deeper into her.

He filled her and then some.

She reached between them and tried to stroke him. But he caught her hand and held her back.

"This is why I needed to tie you up," she mused.

"Then it would have been over already," he said. "And you would have missed all this fun."

She wasn't sure if it was fun or torture. He teased the tension back into her body, teased her to the edge of an orgasm before he pulled out.

She clutched his butt and pushed him back inside her. Then she used her hands to guide his hips.

But he moved again and took her with him as he rolled onto his back. And suddenly she was astride him.

He'd given her the control she'd wanted. And she used it to tease him like he'd teased her, sliding up until his cock nearly came out, then settling back down hard. Up and down...

He groaned and thrashed on the mattress before his hands clutched her hips. He didn't need to guide her.

Muriel knew the rhythm. With him, she could dance. Together they moved as one until she tensed.

Her inner muscles convulsed, her body shuddered, and she screamed his name as an orgasm gripped her.

He was with her, his hands biting into her hips as his body tensed. He shuddered and came, too.

Muriel eased off and dropped onto the mattress on her back, boneless and exhausted. She had needed that. She'd needed him. Completed satiated, she closed her eyes.

But he was already getting out of the bed. She figured he was just cleaning up. But it wasn't the bathroom door she heard opening and closing. It was the front door as he left.

Just as she'd accused him earlier, he was running away. From her? Or from what he felt when they were together?

Muriel wanted to run from those feelings, too. But she wasn't sure she had any muscles left—she was so loose and relaxed—except for the mad pounding of her heart. She was afraid that she was falling for Ronan.

It didn't matter what she felt, though, because Ronan wasn't ever going to let himself feel anything but fear for a relationship. She was going to wind up just like all those other women he'd dated, dumped and left wanting more.

But she realized now, that because of his past, he wasn't capable of giving any more.

CHAPTER TWELVE

RONAN'S HAND SHOOK as he lifted the glass of water to his mouth. "I should have had you guys meet me at the bar," he said. He could have used a stiff drink, instead. But he'd called the meeting in Simon's office, and they all sat around the conference table they used every Tuesday morning for their business meetings.

But it wasn't Tuesday morning.

And this wasn't about business as usual. Of course, ever since he'd been reported to the bar association, it hadn't been business as usual, at least, not for him.

"Do you want a drink?" Simon asked as he stood up and moved toward the bar in the back of his office.

It was Saturday night. Simon should have been with Bette. It was Ronan's fault he wasn't. As if Bette didn't already hate him enough, now she would have another reason. But she wasn't the only one who hated Ronan. Muriel did. And he wasn't too crazy about himself right now, either.

"Pour me a drink," Stone requested. "The trial starts next week."

"Are you ready for it?" Trevor asked him.

"Of course," Stone replied. "I'm just a little worried that I might have some surprises. Like Ronan has."

Ronan had had too many surprises lately.

"Any leads on the mole yet?" Trevor asked Simon.

The managing partner shook his head. "Nothing. I can't figure out who it could be."

And that wasn't good. Simon was the best judge of character of all of them. If he'd been tricked, this mole was good. Very good.

It hadn't taken much to trick Ronan. He'd fallen easily for Arte's bunch of lies. "That's why I called this meeting," he said.

"You know who the mole is?" Simon asked in surprise. Then he sighed. "Don't tell me Muriel Sanz. She doesn't have access to our office."

She'd walked right in one weekend, but Ronan didn't bother sharing that. He didn't believe it was Muriel, either. "I don't know who the mole is, but I'm worried about the practice," he said.

"Why are you worried?" Simon asked.

"I think I'm going to get disbarred," he admitted, and his stomach clenched then sank with the admission.

"You didn't know those witnesses were lying," Stone said. "That'll come out during the investigation of the complaint. You'll be fine."

"Street Legal will be fine," Simon added. Because he was such a good judge of character, he knew that Ronan wasn't worried just about himself.

He wasn't worried just about the practice, either. "I really screwed up," he said.

"The guy's a con artist," Simon reminded him.

He shrugged. "But I took it further than I had to. I used McCann to smear the hell out of Muriel."

Because he'd thought she was like his mother, and he must have subconsciously and childishly been using Muriel to get back at the woman who'd destroyed his father.

"I need to have McCann put out more press releases with the truth about Muriel," he said. It was only fair to undo the damage he'd done.

"Then the bar will think you knew those witnesses were lying," Stone said. "You need to keep your mouth shut and let this play out."

"And keep your zipper up, too," Trevor advised. "It doesn't sound like your plan to seduce her into dropping the complaint worked. Sounds like she seduced you, instead."

She had. He couldn't deny that. But it had made him discover the truth. "I screwed up," he repeated. "And I need to fix it."

"You can," Stone said. "But wait until the complaint has been withdrawn."

"She's not going to withdraw it," Ronan said. And he didn't blame her for not believing him enough to do that. After what he'd done, he would never be able to earn her trust. He, more than anyone, understood how hard it was to trust at all—let alone to trust someone who had already hurt you.

Regret filled him. He was so sorry that he'd hurt her. But sorry wasn't enough.

"So we need to make it go away," Simon said.

And Ronan had an idea about how to do that. "I've got a plan."

"Your last one didn't work," Trevor reminded him. "You should have let *me* seduce her into dropping the complaint. Are you willing to let me try now?"

"No!" Ronan snapped with such force that Stone grabbed his arm, as if he was afraid that Ronan might leap across the table and go for Trevor's throat. He was tempted. But he relaxed back in his chair. "Simon has to do this."

"No," Simon snapped now. "She's Bette's friend. And I'm not cheating on Bette."

"Have her join in," Trevor suggested with a lustful sigh. "That would be fun."

Simon cursed him.

"Two women too much for you to handle?" Trevor teased.

"I can barely handle one," Simon freely admitted.

"This has nothing to do with women," Ronan said. "I want Simon to seduce a man."

"What?" All three of his partners uttered the question.

"Muriel's ex," Ronan said. "He checked you out the other day. I think you could get him talking."

"He's gay?" Trevor asked, his mouth hanging open in shock. "And he was married to The World's Most Beautiful Woman?"

Simon sighed and just murmured, "Con."

"Yes, he is," Ronan said. "And if we can get him to admit that he asked those witnesses to testify and coached them on what to say, I think the bar would throw out the complaint against me."

"I am not going to seduce a man," Simon said.

"You don't have to seduce him," Ronan said. "Just con him."

Simon's blue eyes narrowed.

So Ronan goaded him, "Unless you've lost your touch and aren't up to the task anymore."

Simon cursed him now, but he was grinning. Then he asked, "This isn't just about saving your license or the practice, is it?"

"Of course it is," Ronan said. "What else could it be about?"

"Muriel," Simon replied. "You're falling for her."

Ronan shook his head as panic clutched his heart. That was why he'd run from her apartment the night before—because of the emotions that had rushed through him. He'd wanted to stay; he'd wanted to hold her all night. He'd wanted to wake up and have her face be the first he saw. But it was, anyway; she was forever on his mind.

"No," he said and wished that he sounded as if he meant it. "I am not falling for anyone. I just want to right a wrong." And once that was done, he would forget all about Muriel Sanz. That was the problem. He had to clear his conscience. Then he would be able to get her off his mind and out of his…

Heart?

No. She wasn't in there. No woman had ever been in there.

"I just need for this to be over," he said. And for his life to get back to normal, to picking up women in bars for one-night stands while he focused only on work.

For some reason, normal sounded empty and hollow now.

Muriel's pulse quickened when the doorbell pealed. Had Ronan returned?

She hoped like hell that he had. As wonderful as the night before had been, it had ended too soon. He'd run off too quickly. If he'd stayed…

Hell, if he'd stayed, she would have started getting used to his being around. She would have started envisioning a future with him. And that wasn't possible for so many reasons.

No. It was better that he'd run off. And if she was smart, she wouldn't open the door to him. But she wanted him again—still—so she pulled it open without even looking through the peephole.

But she should have, because if she had, she would have never opened the door. Not to Arte Armand.

That was one man she was never allowing back into her life.

Hell.

But she was so shocked that he'd have the guts to come and see her, that she could say nothing. And apparently, her silence unsettled him because he began to nervously stammer, "Mur-Muriel, I—I know that after everything that happened, you probably don't want to see me."

If he was waiting for her to argue, she couldn't. "No. I don't want to see you." Because now she couldn't see what she once had—the sweet, funny man she'd thought she loved.

She could only see the lying weasel he had become. Or maybe he had always been the lying weasel. How had she been so blind? She closed her eyes now, as just the sight of his ridiculously handsome face made her feel sick. Where Ronan's features could have been carved from granite, Arte's would have been porcelain or some other smooth, flawless material. His features were so perfect that he was more pretty than handsome. Had she been shallow? Had she fallen for his almost pretty good looks without seeing his real character?

What character? During the divorce, it had become clear that he had none.

"I didn't think you'd still be mad," he said, as his lips puckered into a petulant pout.

Was he that oblivious to how much he'd hurt her?

"What?" she asked. "How stupid do you think I am?" She had been pretty stupid to fall for Arte in the first place let alone marry him. But she'd thought the prenup would cover her assets. She hadn't realized someone like Ronan Hall would be able to get so easily around it.

"You're not stupid," Arte said. "You're very smart. You used what happened—all the media attention— to take your career to the next level. You're The World's Most Beautiful Woman."

She flinched. The title had begun to wear on her, especially since she felt she hadn't earned it—not like so many other women out there who'd made smart choices. Not someone like her, who kept going for inappropriate man after inappropriate man.

But he must not have noticed her reaction because he continued, "That just goes to prove that there is no such thing as bad publicity."

Maybe Allison McCann would be able to use that for her next ad campaign for her own business. But no matter what campaign Allison launched, she wasn't getting Muriel's business.

"I didn't need any publicity," she reminded him. Since she was fourteen, she'd always had steady work as a model. Her grandmother had worked as a seamstress for a designer who'd given Muriel her first job.

"I do," Arte said. "I'm producing that musical I always talked about."

She didn't know what he was waiting for—congratulations? She knew the only way he'd managed to produce anything was from taking so much money from her in court.

He smiled like a little boy trying to convince his mother to give him a cookie or maybe a puppy. "And I could use some publicity for it," he said, "so people will come and see it."

He'd taken some money from her but not enough to produce anything on Broadway. So it must have been off-off.

"Is that why you're here?" she asked, as her stomach churned with disgust. "You want me to mention your play?"

"Or you could invest in it."

If anyone deserved a slap in the face, it was her ex. But he didn't inspire any passion in Muriel. Maybe he never really had. Because whatever attraction she'd once felt for him paled into insignificance compared to what she felt for Ronan.

All she could do was laugh in his face. "You're crazy if you think I would help you after what you did." And she pushed the door toward him to shove him back into the hallway.

But he caught the edge of the door and held it. "Please, Muriel."

And she saw the desperation in his eyes. Karma must have finally bitten him in the ass. He was probably on the verge of losing everything he'd taken from her.

"Why don't you go see what Ronan Hall can do for you?" she said. But she only made the suggestion because she wanted to hear what he would say about his former divorce lawyer.

"I already did," Arte admitted. "He said that the settlement was final. I can't get any more money from you." His mouth pulled into that petulant pout again. "Even though all the publicity over the trial has made you even more successful."

And he obviously wanted a cut of it, like he was her agent or something. She felt sick. Why had she not realized what a mercenary little man Arte Armand was? How had she been so fooled?

Because she always tried to see the best in people...unlike Ronan who only saw the worst. Why hadn't he seen Arte for what he was, though?

"No, you can't get anything more from me," she agreed. She would never help this slimy jerk with anything.

"He told me that you filed a complaint against him," Arte continued.

So who had called the meeting between the men? Ronan? Or Arte?

It didn't matter. All that mattered was Muriel finally learning the truth.

"I'll testify against him if you'll give me just a little more money," Arte said. "Or if you don't want to pay me, you could mention the musical in some of your interviews or on your social media."

Her fingers curled into a fist. Maybe instead of slapping him, she should just slug him. But she had to know. "What would you do?"

"I'd claim that he knew those witnesses were lying," Arte said. "That he put them up to it. Isn't that what you want? For him to lose his license?"

She shook her head. "No, Arte. What I want is the truth." But she wasn't sure that he would know what that was, even if it bit him on the ass right next to the teeth marks from karma.

He tensed, as if sensing a trap.

"I'd offer to pay you for it," she said. "But I'd still have no idea if you were telling me the truth or just what you thought I wanted to hear."

So she wasn't going to learn anything from Arte Armand, at least, not anything she could trust.

"I'm good at that," he admitted, "telling people what they want to hear, showing them who they want to see."

She shivered as she realized she hadn't been as stupid as she'd thought she was. She had been played by a master.

And she had a feeling that Ronan had been played, as well—even before Arte confessed, "I knew about Hall's childhood—how his mother cheated on his father."

"How?"

"Social media," Arte told her with a cluck of disapproval that she didn't spend more time on it.

She had never been big on social media. She wasn't the model who took selfies and posted them all over the internet. She left the picture taking to the professionals.

"Some tabloid reporter dug up the scoop about his past," Arte said.

"And you used it?" she asked, totally disgusted that he had preyed on Ronan's past and his pain.

Arte seemed almost proud of what he'd done, though, as he nodded. "I knew he was the only lawyer who could break that prenup you had me sign. But he had to be motivated."

So Arte had motivated him.

"Why?" she asked. "That's what I don't understand. I thought we were friends." They had been—before they'd become husband and wife. They had always been more friends than lovers. And she was beginning to realize why.

"Things just don't happen for me like they do for you," Arte said. "You've never had to work for anything. It just falls in your lap."

The modeling. The notoriety. Even those memos she now realized were forged. Those had just dropped into her lap, as well.

Maybe he was right. But she still wasn't about to forgive him for what he'd done.

"It doesn't excuse what you did," she said.

He sighed. "No. It doesn't." He started to turn away from the door. "I was wrong to come here."

"Yes, you were," she agreed. But she was glad that he had—because now she knew she wasn't the only one he'd played. He'd played Ronan, too. "But you were right about something else."

He turned back toward her.

"There is no such thing as bad publicity," she tossed his words back at him. "So go to the press with your scoop."

His brow furrowed. "What scoop?"

"The truth," she said, as if it should have been obvious. But to a man like Arte, the truth was the last thing that was obvious to him. "Tell them what you did to me."

"Would that make amends to you?"

"You don't care about me," she said. He never had. "But you care about your musical. Get it some attention."

"But I'll be the bad guy," he said, clearly horrified at putting himself in the position he'd forced on her. "People will hate me."

He hadn't minded doing that to her. She grabbed one of the magazines from the narrow foyer table behind the door. Showing the cover to him, she said, "It seems like the media likes rooting for the bad guy lately."

Which was a sad commentary on life.

He took the magazine from her and studied it. But she knew he wasn't seeing her face there. He was seeing his own. He nodded. "You're right… I need to do this."

And she realized now why those witnesses had lied for him. Some people would do anything for even a few minutes of fame. Fortunately for her, in this moment Arte was one of those people.

Finally, he glanced up from the magazine to focus on her real face. "I need to do this for you, too. I am sorry, Muriel."

She doubted it, but she nodded as if she accepted his apology. Then she closed the door on his face and on her past. It was time to let it go. All of it.

Even Ronan. Especially Ronan—because he hadn't let go of his own past yet. It still affected him, still influenced him. He was never going to trust a woman or let one as close as she wanted to be to him. She didn't just want him inside her anymore.

She wanted to be inside him, as well—inside his heart. And she wasn't sure he even had one.

No. It was time to let the past go and Ronan Hall along with it.

CHAPTER THIRTEEN

RONAN STARED AT the screen on Simon's laptop as Arte Armand made a full confession on some internet talk show. "How the hell did you manage that?" he asked.

All those years ago on the streets, he'd known Simon was a good con artist. But so many years had passed since then, he'd figured he might have lost his touch. If anything, Simon had only gotten better. He was in awe and executed a little bow of appreciation and respect.

"Yeah," Trevor chimed in from the other side of the conference table. "What'd you have to do to him to convince him to come clean?"

Simon snorted. "I didn't even meet with him."

"What?" Ronan asked. "That was the plan."

"Your plan," Simon reminded him. "And there was no way it would work."

"Just like your seduction plan," Trevor goaded him.

No. That hadn't worked, either. But he didn't understand.

"Why did Arte do this?"

"Who cares?" Trevor asked. "Now you can have the complaint against you thrown out."

"He doesn't need to," Stone said. "My friend in the bar association said the complaint had already been withdrawn. They sent out a certified letter to notify you of that."

Had Muriel withdrawn it even before she learned the truth? Had she trusted him?

Why? He'd done nothing to earn it.

"This is it," Simon said, as he fiddled with his keyboard. After rewinding a bit of the video, he pushed Play again and Arte's voice cracked out of the speakers.

"I recently saw Muriel," he said.

Ronan flinched, realizing the con had probably gone to her for money. It hadn't mattered to him that Ronan had said he wasn't entitled to any more. Hell, he hadn't been entitled to what he'd already gotten out of her.

Arte continued, "And she made it clear that the only way for me to make up for what I did to her was to tell the truth."

"Wonder if she paid him," Stone murmured.

Ronan cursed at the thought of that con getting another penny out of her. "I sure as hell hope not."

"So, you were lying about your marriage?" the reporter asked Arte.

He chuckled and crossed his legs. "I've been lying about a lot of things."

"But you had witnesses at the trial that testified to the orgies."

"Never happened," Arte said.

"Why would those people lie?" the reporter persisted.

Arte sighed. "I promised them things…like parts in the musical I'm producing." And he began a self-promotion monologue that Simon quickly muted.

"And now we know why he wanted to do the interviews," Stone said. "Free publicity."

It sure as hell wasn't out of any kindness of his heart. Ronan doubted he had one.

"Doesn't matter his reasons," Trevor said. "It gets Ronan off the hook with the bar."

He squirmed slightly in his chair. He really hated sitting. "Yeah, I'm no longer in trouble with the bar, but how does it make the firm look that I was so easily duped?"

He felt like a damn fool for getting played so easily.

Simon shook his head. "You don't think anyone has ever gotten away with lying to a lawyer before this?" He snorted. "People lie all the time."

Not Muriel. She'd been telling him the truth from the very beginning. He should have listened to her. Hell, he never should have taken the case against her.

"I hope not," Stone said. "I hope my client's telling the truth."

"Why do you sound so cynical again?" Trevor asked Simon. "I thought you were all in love."

"I am," Simon freely admitted, when once he would have been embarrassed to confess his feelings—to having feelings. "And Bette would never lie to me. I was talking about clients, about this business."

And all the lawyers nodded in agreement. As they knew, the law was a far cry from black and white. There were so many shades of gray.

"I trusted Bette all along," Simon continued. "She was right about Muriel."

"She was," Ronan agreed. Muriel was as straightforward and honest as her true friend had claimed she was. He could only hope that she would be forgiving, as well.

But could she forgive what he'd done? He didn't think he could forgive himself.

The dressing room lights burned hot and bright above the mirror in front of Muriel. But despite the heat, Muriel shivered. She had been so cold lately—without Ronan's touch, without his kisses and his passion.

Did he know what she'd done? That she'd withdrawn the complaint? Or was he so furious that she'd filed it in the first place that he couldn't forgive her?

The truth was out now—all over social media—and even some of the bricks-and-mortar media outlets had reported about her divorce debacle. Arte was getting all the publicity he'd wanted.

She couldn't help but think he'd been wrong about there being no such thing as bad publicity. The public backlash had not been kind to him, threatening to shut down his musical before it even opened.

And there had even been threats of legal action, of charges being brought against him and his friends for lying under oath.

Muriel should have felt vindication. Her apartment looked like a funeral parlor again with all the *I'm sorry* flower arrangements. Everyone had apologized to her for believing her ex's lies.

Everyone but Ronan...

She hadn't seen him in over a week—since that night he'd run from her bedroom right after they'd had sex. Maybe wanting to tie him up had scared him off.

She would have expected a man like Ronan— notorious for his sexual prowess—would have loved a little sexual play. But apparently that was only if he was in control.

Was that why he'd run out? Because he'd been afraid he was losing control...?

Was he starting to have feelings for her, too?

Or was she only fooling herself like she had with Arte? He certainly had never been really interested in her—just in her money.

She sighed and made a face at her reflection in the mirror. The shoot was over. She had nothing she needed to change into—no hair or makeup to do.

In fact, from how quiet the photo studio had become, she suspected everyone had left but her. That was good. If there were reporters waiting outside, they might have given up by now. When everyone else left, they'd probably thought she sneaked out somehow. And she should have.

But she hadn't wanted to go home to that flower shop. She could have called Bette to meet her somewhere. Or she could have gone out with some of the other models who'd invited her along to dinner and drinks.

Her stomach growled. And she regretted refusing their invitation. But she hadn't been very hungry lately. At least, not for food.

She was hungry for Ronan. For even just a glimpse of him.

The press had been hounding him, too, and they'd caught him outside the office of Street Legal. He'd looked so damn handsome even as he'd lowered his head and ducked into a waiting limo without commenting to reporters.

What could he say?

That he'd been wrong?

Would a man like Ronan—a man that stubborn and proud—ever admit that he had been wrong?

She had been wrong, too, though, and she hadn't contacted him. Who was the coward now? Or maybe she was so used to things just falling in her lap, like Arte had pointed out, that she expected Ronan to do the same?

She sighed and glanced into the mirror again. And this time it wasn't her face she saw in the glass. It was his...

She met his reflection's dark-eyed gaze and asked, "What are you doing here?"

"Waiting for you to be done," he said. "Everyone else left."

"You were here for the shoot?" she asked. "I didn't see you." And she looked for him at every one of them, hoping he'd show up like he had that once.

"I couldn't watch," he said.

She turned toward him then. "Why not?" This shoot hadn't been for Bette's Beguiling Bows. It was a perfume campaign. She had been wearing an evening gown instead of lingerie.

"I couldn't watch another man touch you," he said. A muscle twitched along his tightly clenched jaw, and he spoke through gritted teeth. "Like that model was touching you..."

She laughed at his outlandish claim. "You were jealous?" She couldn't believe that a man with Ronan's confidence would ever be jealous of another man.

Unless he still believed all those lies about her. Didn't he think Arte had finally told the truth?

"Is that what this is?" he asked, as if he had a horrible taste in his mouth. "I've never felt like this before."

"Why not?" she asked.

"Because I never cared."

It wasn't a declaration of love. But coming from Ronan , it was nearly as monumental. Muriel's heart rate quickened, and it was suddenly hard to breathe. She parted her lips to drag in some air.

And then his mouth was there, moving hungrily over hers. He kissed her as if he was consuming her, his lips and teeth nibbling at hers. He suddenly pulled back and uttered a deep groan.

"Why do you affect me like no one else ever has?" he asked her.

She could have asked him the same question, but she just smiled with the pleasure his comment gave her. Even if she followed the cardinal rule of gossip and only believed half of what she'd heard, he'd had a lot of lovers. So it was good to know that she was special to him.

"You don't have to be jealous because of me," she assured him. "Because you're the only man I want."

He tensed, and she saw that look of fear pass through his dark eyes. Instead of her words reassuring him, she'd scared him. And she remembered he was a man who would never let himself fall in love— because he didn't want to wind up like his father.

But she was not like his mother. And she wanted him to know that. "I only sleep with one man at a time," she said. "And you're the only man I want to sleep with now."

Yet they had never slept together. He always took off right after they had sex.

"Is that why you withdrew your complaint?" he asked.

She shook her head. "Sorry, you did not seduce me into that."

"Why did you do it then?" he asked.

"Because Arte told me the truth."

"And the rest of the world, too," Ronan remarked. He studied her face. "How did you get him to do that?"

She shrugged. "He must have realized it was the only publicity he was going to get."

"It's bad."

"Yes," she said. "Is it for you? Have you had any backlash?"

"The guys have called me an idiot," he said. "But it hasn't affected the practice any. In fact, I think it's brought in more clients."

"So you've been busy?" she asked. And now she was fishing to see where he'd been, why he hadn't been around. He wasn't the only one experiencing jealousy for the first time.

He nodded. "And I wasn't sure you'd want to see me after the truth finally came out. Or if you'd hit me again like you did in that first elevator…"

She laughed and reaching up, pressed her lips to his cheek. "Poor baby…"

"I had it coming," he said. "I'm sorry."

"Arte duped you—just like he did me," she said. And somehow that made her feel better about it. If a man as brilliant as Ronan had been fooled, she didn't feel like such a fool herself.

Ronan flinched. He obviously hadn't liked being conned. "There was more to it than that."

"I know." But she didn't want to talk about the past now. She'd missed him too much. And her body ached for his.

But she turned away from him, to face the mirror again. Over her shoulder, his reflection's eyes narrowed as he studied her.

"Muriel...?"

Since she'd had to give back the gown she'd worn for the photo shoot, she wore only a robe now. She'd been too lethargic—from all the sleepless nights thinking about him—that she hadn't worked up the energy to change into her street clothes. They overflowed the top of her bag, which sat on the floor beneath the long dressing room table.

Watching him in the mirror, she untied the sash of her robe and pulled it through the loops.

His mouth curved into a slight grin, and he told her, "You are not going to tie me up."

"No," she agreed. "I want you to touch me." She parted the robe and let it drop from her shoulders so that she stood naked before the mirror and him. "I want you to touch me here."

She pressed her fingers to her lips and swiped her

tongue across the tips. Then she glided those wet fingertips down her throat and over the curve of one breast. She touched the already taut nipple, stroking her wet fingertip across it. And a moan slipped through her lips. "I really want you to touch me here…"

But it seemed as if he was paralyzed as he just stood behind her and watched as she touched herself.

She guided her hand over her stomach, which, thanks to him stealing her appetite away, was flatter than it had ever been. Then she raked her nails over her mound until she could slide her fingers between her inner lips. She gasped.

And Ronan echoed that gasp. A groan tore from his throat, and his paralysis ended as he reached for her. "Doesn't look like you need me," he murmured as he placed his hands on her shoulders and met her gaze in the mirror.

"Looks can be deceiving," she told him, knowing they were both well aware of that now. Then she assured him, "I do need you." And she placed her hands over his on her shoulders and guided them down to her breasts.

They watched each other in the mirror. She watched him play with her breasts, tease her nipples into even tighter points as tension wound inside her. And with every whimper and moan she uttered, his eyes got darker, his gaze more intense, and behind her she could feel the heat and hardness of his body. His erection throbbed against her bottom.

He wanted—needed—her just as badly as she did him. At least, that was what she tried to convince herself of as her desire for him slipped into madness. She tried to turn around, but he held her the way they were—her back to his front—and he continued to watch her in the mirror even as he undid his pants and freed his cock.

She could feel the slick bare skin of his dick rubbing against her ass now. Then latex separated skin from skin as he rolled on a condom.

Fortunately he seemed as staunch a supporter of safe sex as she had always been. So maybe—someday— they could try it without the condom. But that implied a commitment she wasn't sure either of them was ready to make.

Right now, all she expected from him was pleasure. And he gave that to her. Leaning over her shoulder, he kissed her neck. She turned her head until lips met lips. They kissed hungrily. She was so thirsty for him, on fire with a thirst only he could quench.

Then his hands moved to her waist and he lifted her onto the makeup counter so she knelt with her head toward the mirror and her ass toward him. He moved his fingers into her before leaning over and lapping at her with his tongue. He licked her so sexily— as he watched her in the mirror—that she came. A little squeal of surprise slipped through her lips over how quickly the orgasm took her.

He grinned at her. But then the grin disappeared as his control snapped. And he moved between her legs, guiding himself inside her.

She gasped again as he filled her. Every time it was a surprise that they fit. But they did fit, so well that it was as if they were made for each other. And even though days had passed since they'd had sex last, they moved together in that perfectly choreographed dance like they'd been doing it for years.

As he thrust inside her, his hands found her breasts again. He cupped the mounds, but they overflowed his palms. So he focused on the nipples, gently twisting and teasing them as he built the tension inside her again.

She felt as if she might split in two—not from his size or thrusts, but from the unbearable need for release. He moved one hand from her breasts and stroked his thumb over her clit.

And she came again, a scream tearing from her throat that she couldn't stop. The release shuddered through her with such intensity that tears streaked down her cheeks and her body shook in reaction.

Hopefully everyone had left because if they hadn't, someone would probably have called the police to report an attack. She'd sounded like she was being murdered.

Then Ronan tensed and shouted out her name as

he came, leaning his head, hair slick with perspiration, against her back. He uttered a ragged sigh. "You are so damn incredible…"

She wasn't, but what happened between them was. It had started with just an attraction, one that they hadn't been able to overcome despite their anger and mistrust. And every time they came together it was more powerful than the last. The attraction wasn't dying off; it was only getting more and more intense.

Ronan must have realized it, too, because when he lifted his head from her back, she caught a glimpse of his eyes in the mirror. And she saw the fear in them.

But she didn't know if that fear was his or hers. Because she felt it, too. She was afraid that she was falling for a man who would never let himself love anyone.

She was glad he'd found her here instead of her apartment because now she was the one who wanted to run. But she wasn't sure where she could go to escape these feelings for him—feelings that were overwhelming her.

CHAPTER FOURTEEN

Ronan glanced at the address Muriel had texted him on his cell. Was this right?

This small house in the Bronx was where she'd wanted him to meet her. But why?

This wasn't her place. Was it some kind of S and M sex den? She seemed to really want to tie him up. He wasn't sure if he should ring the doorbell or not. But a barking dog from within the modest house must have alerted her to his arrival because she opened the door and smiled at him.

"You came."

Standing two steps down on the stoop made him level with her beautiful face. He closed the distance between them and kissed her, and as he did, he murmured against her lips, "Not yet. But I want to come soon…inside you…"

Her face flushed and her pupils dilated, swallowing the green the way he wanted to swallow her—

"Is your friend here?" a male voice asked from within the house.

And Ronan tensed.

"Muriel, bring him in," a female voice chimed into the conversation.

And Ronan wondered if Arte and his friends had really lied about the orgies.

"Where am I?" he asked her. And why had she had him meet her here?

"Home," she said, and her smile widened.

"You bought a house?" he asked. With the money she had to be making as The World's Most Beautiful Woman, she could have easily afforded something much nicer than this.

She laughed. "No. This is my grandparents' house," she said. "Home..."

That explained why she was there. But why had she invited him? "Did you want me to meet you here?" he asked. Maybe he'd misunderstood the text. Maybe she'd just been telling him where she was because he'd asked her if she was home. He took a step down. "I can leave."

"No," she said, and she tugged him back up the stairs. "I invited you here. I wanted you to come for Sunday dinner."

His breath caught, panic pressing on his chest as he stepped over that threshold. And it wasn't just because he wasn't fond of little dogs like the one that had rushed down the hall to bounce around his feet. It was because he didn't like families.

Any families...

He'd hated his own, and he'd never seen another

one he'd wanted to be part of, even the ones that had seemed perfect on the outside. Pitching his voice low, he asked, "Why would you invite me here?"

Hurt flashed through her green eyes. "I wanted you to meet them."

"You should have asked if I'd wanted to meet them," he said.

"I didn't care," she replied, and there was a sharp tone to her voice now. "I wanted you to see why I was so upset about the trial. I wanted you to understand."

And suddenly he did. He hadn't been certain if she'd forgiven him, not even though they'd had sex every day since that night in the dressing room. A couple of weeks had passed, which was a long time for him. Longer than he'd seen any other woman exclusively.

This might have been the point in a relationship where the woman introduced the man to her family. But he didn't know, because he'd never been in a relationship. And it didn't sound as if he was really in one now.

Muriel obviously hadn't forgiven him yet. Not that he could blame her.

"So this is an ambush?" he asked, keeping his voice low so her grandparents wouldn't overhear. "They have to hate me just as much as you did."

Or did she still?

"I explained to them what Arte did," she said, "how he lied to you, too."

He nodded but he wasn't convinced that was really an excuse for what he'd done to her. So he didn't
expect her grandparents to be forgiving or sweet. But
he didn't turn for the door and run like he wanted.

However they treated him, he deserved it. And
maybe when Muriel saw how her family couldn't forgive him, she would realize that she and Ronan had
no possibility of a future together.

The silence unnerved Muriel. It was the first that had
fallen since she and Ronan had left Papa and Nana's
house. All through dinner conversation had flowed
easily. Ronan had charmed. Nana had flirted. Papa
had teased.

It was the most fun Muriel had had in such a long
time. And she'd thought Ronan had enjoyed himself.
He'd eaten. He'd drunk. He'd laughed. He'd grinned.

But he had never looked at her.

Was he furious?

She had kind of ambushed him. But if she'd told
him that address was her grandparents', he never
would have showed up. So she'd tricked him.

"I'm sorry," she said. "I should have told you." She
glanced at him across the console that separated the
driver and passenger seats.

"You should have asked me," he corrected her. But
he didn't take his gaze from the road. And his hands
gripped the steering wheel tightly.

"You would have said no," she replied.

"Yes, I would have," he said. And now he glanced across at her, and there was sadness and regret in his dark eyes. "I'm not the kind of man women take home to meet their families."

Heat flushed her face. "I told you that's not why I invited you," she said. "I wanted you to see why I was so upset with you."

"Because of how all that media attention affected them."

She nodded. "They had reporters camped out on their stoop, asking them horribly intrusive questions about me, about my life and upbringing."

"Why are they the ones who raised you?" he asked. "You've never said how they came to be your legal guardians."

She'd fallen into their laps just as so much had fallen into hers. She sighed. "My mother was very young when she got pregnant with me. Just a teenager who'd fallen for an older boy. He left for the Marines, and she had me. But he didn't come back."

"I'm sorry," he said and reached across the console for her hand.

But she pulled it back. She didn't need comforting. "He didn't die," she said. "He just didn't come back to the Bronx. And when my mother realized he wasn't coming back, she wanted to leave, too. She wanted to go to college, so my grandparents said they would take care of me."

"But she never came back, either?" he asked.

"No. She moved to the West Coast. She sends cards and letters and calls sometimes. But Papa and Nana, they're my parents. The people I love the most and who love me most."

"Why did you want me to see that?" he asked. "So I would apologize again?" He had—to her grandparents—repeatedly. "I already told you I was wrong. What more do you want from me?"

His heart. She wanted his heart. But she knew it wasn't something he was going to freely offer her. It wasn't going to just land in her lap like everything else in her life had. She would have to work to earn it.

"I wanted you to see that I'm not a horrible person," she told him. "I don't go around slapping people and filing complaints and…"

"Having sex in elevators?" he asked when she trailed off. And she heard the humor in his voice now.

"No," she said. "Except for you, I've never done any of that stuff."

"I know that," he said. "Well, not the elevator stuff but the rest of it."

It hadn't hurt that her grandparents had gone on and on about what a sweet, down-to-earth person she was. But a man like Ronan wouldn't want sweet and down-to-earth. He'd want the passionate woman from the elevator.

Maybe having him meet Papa and Nana had been a huge mistake. Maybe he would never look at her the way he had before…with such lust.

She reached over the console and slid her hand over his thigh. The muscles rippled and tensed beneath her touch, and something long and hard swelled against the fly of his jeans.

"Muriel…" His voice held a warning, one she ignored as she slid her hand higher up his thigh and then over his fly. "Do you want me to crash this car?"

She didn't want to crash but she did want him to lose control. Hell, she just wanted him. It didn't matter how much sex they had; she was always hungry for more and the pleasure only he was able to give her.

"You're a good driver," she said.

He chuckled. "You've never ridden with me before."

No. Despite the amount of time they'd spent together the past couple of weeks, they hadn't done much but sex. They hadn't gone out to dinner. They always ordered in. They hadn't seen a show or a concert. Their only entertainment had been each other.

Since she'd been hiding out from all the reporters hounding her, she had been fine with keeping things private between them. But the press wasn't bothering her nearly as much as they had.

Now they could go out in public. But instead of heading toward the city, Ronan pulled his vehicle off into a small wooded area. The two-track road he'd found might once have led somewhere, but nobody had traveled it in a while. Weeds had nearly overgrown it. He didn't drive very far, though, just far enough that the car wouldn't be seen from the street. Then he put the car into Park and shut off the ignition.

Muriel knew why he'd stopped—what he wanted. She wanted it, too. So she pushed her other concerns aside and focused only on the overwhelming attraction between them.

He pushed back his seat and lifted her across the console, and now there was nothing between them. But he settled her onto his lap so that she was staring out the windshield, too. The woods were getting dark, and the glass just reflected back their images—like that mirror in the dressing room.

And like with that mirror in the dressing room, they watched each other, watched every flicker of pleasure and sigh of desire through parted lips. She wore a dress today, one so short that it had already ridden up around her waist. Ronan pushed her panties aside to slide his fingers inside her. Then he moved his other hand farther up beneath her dress and pushed up her strapless bra to free her breasts. While he played with the nipple of one breast, he slid his fingers in and out of her. Soon Muriel was panting for air, and the windows fogged up. She couldn't see herself anymore. She couldn't see Ronan.

She could only feel him as he lowered his fly, sheathed himself and slid it inside her. He lifted her so that she could slide down on top of him. He filled her completely, perfectly.

The tension inside her spiraled up, then broke, and

she shuddered as she came. He tensed and writhed beneath her, losing control until he came, too, and shouted her name. Limp with release, Muriel sagged against the steering wheel and the horn blew.

Ronan cursed and pulled her back. "Damn, someone might see us."

Moments ago her control had snapped. Now her temper did. "And why would that be so terrible?" she asked. "Are you afraid of being seen with me?"

"What are you talking about?" he asked.

Muriel straightened her clothes and scrambled back into the passenger seat. "I'm talking about how you never take me anywhere, how we're never out in public." And as the words reverberated inside the steamed up car, Muriel winced, recognizing that she sounded like a nagging wife.

"You haven't been really happy with the publicity I already got for you," he said. "So I hardly thought you'd want to be seen with me."

And she winced again because he had a valid point. The press had just begun to die down. If she was seen in public with her ex's divorce lawyer, she would stir up the scandal all over again.

Then he continued, "It's not as if we're dating, anyway."

And she felt as if he'd punched her. "What are we doing?" she asked. But the question was more for her than him.

He knew what he was doing—what he was always doing—just screwing around…

She didn't screw around; she fell in love. And once again she'd picked the wrong man to fall in love with. At least Ronan hadn't conned her. He'd been honest from the start that he wasn't the forever kind of guy.

For a man who knew what he was doing, he didn't give her an answer—just opened and closed his mouth as if he couldn't find the words.

"I'm sorry," she said.

"You're sorry?"

She nodded. "I shouldn't have asked you to drive me home—now you have no place to escape."

His brow furrowed with confusion. "What are you talking about?"

"How you always take off and run the minute we're done having sex," she explained. "You can't do that now. Unless you toss me out of the car and have me walk to the city."

"I wouldn't do that," he said. But he started up the car and backed quickly onto the street. He began to drive so fast that it was clear he couldn't wait to escape.

"I shouldn't have brought you to meet my grand-parents," she said. "I guess I was hoping you'd see that they have something special, that not every marriage is like your parents'."

"Most of them are," he insisted. "How can you forget I'm a divorce lawyer?"

"I didn't forget," she assured him. "But you have to realize you're only seeing the bad marriages. Not the good ones."

He snorted derisively. "I could read you statistics, too. But I wouldn't have thought I'd have to. Your marriage was a scam. How could you ever consider getting married again?" He shivered as if he abhorred the thought.

"I didn't think I would, either," she admitted. "Arte made me doubt my judgment, not just in men but in friends, too. But then Bette became such a good, loyal friend to me." She blinked as tears stung her eyes. She'd learned that the quantity of friends didn't matter; it was the quality.

"I've been lucky in that regard, too," Ronan said. "I have damn good friends."

"So, if we can choose good friends, why can't we choose good mates?" she asked.

He glanced over at her then looked back at the road. "I don't want a mate," he said. "I never intend to get married. If you thought taking me to meet your grandparents would make me propose."

She snorted now. "God, no. I don't want to marry you. We haven't even been out on an actual date." And that was what she'd wanted from him. Not a proposal—just a date. An actual relationship and the hope that it could go somewhere, someday, when they were both ready.

But it was clear that Ronan would never be ready. At least, not with her.

They were silent the rest of the drive into the city. And when he drew near her apartment building, he double parked by a cab. He obviously had no intention of showing her to her door. She jumped out before he could even put the vehicle into Park.

"Don't worry," she told him. "I have no intention of trying to tie you up or down."

"Muriel…"

"In fact, consider yourself cut loose right now, for good," she said as she slammed the passenger door shut.

He opened his door and called out to her over the roof of the car. "Muriel!"

She sucked in a breath to brace herself before turning back toward him and the car.

His brow furrowed. "I don't understand. I thought you were enjoying…" He glanced around the busy street as if worried someone might overhear them.

But everyone appeared too busy with their own lives to bother eavesdropping on theirs. And for once there were no reporters around.

She was old news again. And, unfortunately, so was whatever the hell they'd been doing. "I'm not enjoying it anymore."

It hurt—every time he ran away from her, it hurt. So this time she was the one who turned and ran…

But she knew it wouldn't matter how far and fast

she went. The pain was going to catch up with her. She had fallen in love with another man who would never be able to love her back.

CHAPTER FIFTEEN

"ARE YOU SURE she wants me here?" Ronan asked, as he stood in front of the last empty chair near the stage runway. It was probably the only empty chair in the whole, crowded, loud, chaotic place. He was lucky Simon had saved it for him. But he wasn't certain he should have.

"Who?" Simon asked. "Muriel?"

Her name struck him like a blow, making his breath shudder out in a ragged sigh.

"Don't worry," Simon said. "Muriel has no idea you're here."

He didn't doubt that or he probably wouldn't have made it past security even with the pass Simon had given him and the other partners. Trevor and Stone sat on the other side of their managing partner.

"I was talking about Bette," Ronan said. "She's not exactly a fan of mine, and this is her show." The official launch of her line of lingerie. She'd worked very hard for this, and he didn't want to mess it up.

"Maybe if you become a fan of hers, she'll become one of yours," Simon suggested.

Ronan settled onto the chair next to him. "I'm already a fan," he said. "Huge, huge fan of her work."

And Simon chuckled. "So you've seen some of her designs already…" Then he nodded. "Of course, when you were seducing Muriel."

He wasn't sure he'd ever actually seduced her. But she had definitely seduced him—so much so that he couldn't stop wanting her.

It had been almost two weeks since she'd dumped him outside her apartment building. Dumped? They'd never really been together for her to be able to dump him. Like she'd said, they'd never gone out on a real date. He should have taken her. Or at least asked… instead of just assuming that she wouldn't want to be seen with him.

Because then she'd gotten the wrong idea about him, had thought he was ashamed of her or something.

But that wasn't the only wrong idea. She'd started to think that he might be looking for more than just sex. And that was crazy.

Of course he'd had fun with her no matter what they'd been doing. And he'd really enjoyed that dinner with her grandparents. They were as sweet and funny and honest as she was.

Fingers snapped in front of his face. "What's wrong with you?" Trevor asked from where he leaned around Simon.

"He zoned out thinking about Muriel," Simon said as if he perfectly understood.

Stone snorted. "Just because you do that thinking about Bette doesn't mean Ronan is falling in love, too."

Trevor laughed. "Ronan in love...that would be the day."

"Why?" Ronan asked, and even he was surprised to hear how defensive he sounded. "Why would that be the day?"

Stone stood and stared down at him, his gray eyes full of concern. "Are you okay?"

No. He hadn't been since Muriel had gotten out of the car that day and told him she was cutting him loose.

"You're the one who always says love is a sham," Trevor reminded him. "So of course you're never falling in love."

"I used to say that, too," Simon said. "Now I know the truth."

So did Ronan. The truth was that Muriel was a good person. She was not a cheater or a liar. She was not his mother. And he had been an idiot to ever think she was.

"Love is real, guys," Simon said.

While Stone and Trevor laughed, Ronan did not—because, for the first time, he realized that it was.

Simon loved Bette and she loved him. Sure, maybe they wouldn't last. Maybe they'd burn out like so many other couples did—except for Muriel's grand-parents. They still flirted with each other, still snuck hot glances and touched each other—and they were old. They'd been together so many years, but they still saw each other. It was possible to love someone and it was possible for that love to last.

He didn't know if it would for him. But maybe he owed it to himself, and to Muriel, to at least try. He knew that it would take more than flowers and a din-ner invitation to get her to give him another chance, though. It was going to take a grand gesture—one that would be humbling and humiliating if she didn't want him anymore.

If she'd moved on to someone else…

He opened his mouth to ask Simon if Muriel was seeing anyone, but before he could get the question out, the lights dimmed and the background music stopped playing. With a swish, the curtains opened to a woman standing behind a podium. Bette wore one of her own designs—a silk robe with bows—and for the first time, Ronan understood why his partner was so crazy about his former assistant.

She was gorgeous. But she wasn't The World's Most Beautiful Woman.

Bette was talking, but he couldn't hear any of it. He couldn't hear anything but his pulse pounding in his ears and his blood rushing through his veins—because Muriel had stepped onto the stage.

She looked gorgeous in a soft pink teddy with

bows as the straps. Even her slippers, as she glided down the runway, had bows on them. He wanted her to see him. But anytime she looked away from the stage, so many bulbs flashed that she was probably blinded.

Did every fashion show get this much attention or were they here for Muriel?

He couldn't blame them. That was why he was here. Sure, he'd claimed he was just supporting Bette. But he'd wanted to see Muriel again.

But seeing was never enough…

He wanted to kiss her and touch her and taste her. And most of all, he wanted to hold her, all night long—he wouldn't run away.

He had to convince her to give him another chance. And as the bulbs continued to flash all around her, he realized exactly how he was going to do it. Yeah, he'd be humiliated if it failed. But another chance with Muriel far outweighed any risk of humiliation.

Spots danced in front of Muriel's eyes. She was lucky she hadn't fallen during the show. All those flashing bulbs had nearly blinded her. She wasn't able to see well. But she'd been able to feel…his presence.

Ronan had attended the show.

Before giving tickets to Simon's business partners, Bette had asked if it was okay with Muriel. She'd agreed, but only because she hadn't thought Ronan would actually attend.

Had he been alone? Or had he brought a date? Someone he wanted to be seen with?

Of course, he'd explained why he'd never taken her out. But the press had let up on her; they could have taken their relationship public. But then, it had only ever been sex, and taking that public—more public than the elevator, the dressing room and the car— would have gotten them arrested.

Muriel stepped out of the dressing room where she'd changed from Bette's Beguiling lingerie into a short black dress and boots. She'd promised Bette she would attend her party after the show. But if Ronan was there…

Bulbs flashed in her face again, and she flinched. Ronan was the least of her concerns at the moment. Along with the cameras, there were microphones—all shoved toward her face. How had they gotten backstage?

"What do you have to say about the latest news?" someone asked.

Muriel wasn't sure what they meant, but she focused on what they should be focused on. "Bette's brilliant," she said. "Her designs are amazing. And she's the one you should be interviewing." Not her. She had had more than enough press to last her a lifetime.

"So you have nothing to say about the interview your ex gave?" a woman reporter asked.

She swallowed a groan. What had Arte done now?

The man was seriously a pathetic fame whore. "I didn't see his interview," she said, "and I don't care to."

"So he's right—nothing he says or does will compel you to give him another chance?"

"God, no." She shuddered at the thought. What the hell kind of game was Arte playing now?

Did he think declarations of undying love for her would save his musical?

The last thing Muriel wanted to do was feed his need for fame. She shook her head. "You're wasting your time. And so is he. Please focus on the real story and Bette's beautiful designs."

Taking her advice, the reporters put down the microphones and turned away with the cameras. As she did, the female reporter shook her head. "You're a stronger woman than I am, then," she murmured. "There's no way in hell I would say no to Ronan Hall."

Muriel reached out and grasped her arm, jerking the woman to a halt. She waited until the others had filed out of the hallway before asking, "What? What did you say about Ronan?"

"He's the one who did all the talking," the woman said. "About you."

"He—he's the ex you're talking about?"

The woman nodded then laughed. "You thought I was talking about your ex-husband?"

"Yes."

"Hell, no, I was talking about his gorgeous lawyer. Nobody even knew the two of you were dating until he gave the interview at the fashion show."

Muriel hadn't even known they were dating. "He—he told you that?"

"I can show you the interview," the woman offered.

The woman pulled a tablet from her bag and touched the screen. A video began to play. The woman spoke on camera—to Ronan. "You've declined all interviews about representing Arte Armand in his divorce trial from Muriel Sanz. Why have you agreed to talk now?"

"Because I need to publicly apologize to Muriel," he said. "I had no idea her ex had influenced those witnesses to perjure themselves."

"Yet someone reported you to the bar association for suborning perjury," the reporter said on the tablet.

Muriel glanced at the young woman. She wasn't a normal tabloid reporter. She was good.

"That person was misinformed," Ronan said, "and later withdrew her complaint."

"Was that person Muriel Sanz?" the reporter asked.

Ronan offered the reporter a grin and a redirection. "I want to talk more about Muriel," he said. "I want to talk about how beautiful and honest and hardworking she is."

"You sound like a man in love," the reporter remarked. In real life, however, she was focused on Muriel's face instead of the screen.

Muriel felt her watching, but her attention was on the tablet, on Ronan's unfairly handsome face. She looked for fear or panic. But she saw nothing except another grin cross his face.

"I guess I do…" he murmured.

"Are you in love with Muriel Sanz?"

"I was falling for her," he said.

"You were dating Muriel Sanz?"

They hadn't actually been dating, but he nodded as if they had been.

"I blew it, though," he said.

The reporter giggled on camera, and standing next to Muriel, her face flushed with embarrassment. "I find that hard to believe, Mr. Hall…"

"No," he said, his voice gruff with regret.

Or was that just wishful thinking on Muriel's part? Did she want him to regret having run away again?

Actually, she was the one who'd run last. But he hadn't stopped her. Then. What the hell was he up to now?

"I really screwed up," he said. "I don't think there's anything I can do that will convince her to give me another chance."

On the tablet, the reporter reached out and grasped his arm. "I'm sure you'll come up with something—" her fingers stroked his arm "—or someone."

Muriel looked at the reporter now—in real life

standing next to her. And she had no doubt that she now knew what jealousy felt like...

Because she wanted to claw out the woman's eyes.

"Hey, he didn't take me up on it," the reporter assured Muriel. "Like I could seriously compete with The World's Most Beautiful Woman."

"There is no competition," she assured the reporter. Because despite what he'd claimed in that interview, there was nothing between her and Ronan anymore. There had never been anything real between them.

Just sex...

She missed that—so much—missed how he'd kissed her and touched her and stroked her.

She missed him, too, though. She missed his smart-ass remarks and his stubbornness and even his fear...

She'd caught a glimpse of that fear at the end of the interview—when he'd said he didn't think there was anything he could do to convince her to give him a second chance.

But if he'd really wanted one, why hadn't he just asked her?

Why had he stayed away these past couple of weeks?

Hadn't he missed her like she'd missed him?

"I am not competing for Ronan Hall," she told the reporter.

"So, you're saying I can have him?" the woman asked—hopefully.

She didn't think anyone could really have Ronan— not for long and never for keeps. She wasn't going to risk her heart. Not again…

CHAPTER SIXTEEN

FOR THE FIRST time in his life, Ronan understood what it meant to fail epically. His hand shook as he clicked off the flat-screen TV that was mounted over his white marble fireplace. He turned toward the windows that looked out over Central Park. He'd seen enough of the news broadcast.

The reporters had ambushed Muriel outside the door of her dressing room at the show. Since she'd been so surprised, she had spoken honestly.

She wasn't going to give him another chance.

God, no...

That had been her reply. He felt sick and hollow inside—even more than he had when he'd dropped her off that night. He missed her so damn much.

Apparently he was just going to have to get used to it, though. She wasn't giving him a second chance.

His doorbell rang, echoing off the high, coffered ceilings of his apartment. He hesitated before heading toward the door. It was probably one of his partners or maybe all of them. Except for Simon.

He would be celebrating with Bette. Her fashion show had been a huge success. But, of course, her designs couldn't help but look amazing when The World's Most Beautiful Woman was modeling them.

The bell rang again—longer and louder this time—as if someone was repeatedly stabbing the button. Irritated now, he stalked toward the door and jerked it open. "What the hell—"

But it wasn't Trevor or Stone standing in the hall outside his penthouse apartment.

"Muriel," he murmured, shocked to see her. How had she even found him? He had never brought her back to his place. He should have...

But then, he would have found it even harder to sleep in his bed if she'd ever been in it with him. Not that he'd been sleeping, anyway.

He couldn't do anything but think about her—how she'd felt, how she'd tasted.

"Muriel," he murmured again as he reached for her. But before he could wrap his arms around her, she slapped her palms against his chest and shoved him back, just as she had shoved him out of her apartment that one night. But now she was shoving her way inside. After stepping through his door, she slammed it shut behind herself. "What the hell are you up to now?" she demanded.

"Up to?" he asked. "What do you mean?"

"That interview you gave," she said. "Was that to appease your conscience?"

"You once told me that I don't have one to appease," he reminded her.

"Then why did you do it?" she asked, and her gorgeous green eyes narrowed with suspicion. "Why the hell would you give an interview and open everything up again?"

He flinched as he realized now what a bad idea it had been. "Everybody else sends you flowers," he said. "Your place already looks like a funeral parlor."

She glared at him but she didn't argue about the flowers. Instead, a little glint lit up her eyes. "If you'd wanted to send something, there's chocolate or wine."

He slapped his forehead. "Chocolate or wine... I didn't think of those things."

"You went straight for the news interview instead," she said. "And I'm still trying to figure out why."

At the moment, so was he.

She had once seemed offended that he hadn't taken their relationship public. He couldn't have taken it any more public than he just had. Except it was obviously too little, too late. They had no relationship, so the only thing that had gone public was his humiliation when she'd made it clear that she was not going to give him another chance.

He expelled a ragged sigh. "It wasn't a smart move," he admitted, "but I did it because, just like I told those reporters, I have fallen for you."

She closed her eyes, as if she couldn't even look at him, and murmured, "I wish you would have told me first."

He tensed. Was that because she didn't return his

feelings? "So did I make a fool of myself?" he wondered. Not that he cared about his pride. He didn't care about anything but her.

She shook her head, tumbling her long wavy hair around her shoulders. He loved when she did that when she was naked and astride him. "No. I just wish you'd told me…"

Oh, no. She had moved on—she was dating someone else already. And probably really dating him, like dinner and movies and shows and art galleries…

"So I'm too late?" he asked. "You're already seeing somebody el—"

"No!" she exclaimed as she opened her eyes. "I am not seeing anyone."

"But you don't want to see me again," he said.

Her brow furrowed with confusion. "I never said that."

"Yes, you did," he said, and he pointed toward the dark television screen. "I believe your words were *God, no* when asked if you would ever give me another chance."

"I thought the ex they were talking about was Arte," she said.

The tightness in his chest eased, and he sighed out his relief. "Okay, that makes sense."

"I didn't even know you were my ex," she said. "We were never really together."

"We were lovers," he said. In more ways than he knew because he had fallen in love with her. Of course, he hadn't realized it at the time because he'd never been in love before.

Her green eyes gleamed as if she was remembering all those times they'd been together...

And hope flared inside him. "I know you won't give Arte another chance. But what about me? Will you give me another chance, or did I completely blow it?"

She narrowed her eyes and studied his face. "Is that what you want?" she asked. "To date me or for me to blow you?"

He chuckled. "I'd be lying if I didn't say both."

She laughed, too.

But she hadn't answered his question or commented on his feelings. Did she have any for him?

"What do you want, Muriel?" he asked her. And this time when he stepped toward her, she didn't push him back. She let him close his hands over her shoulders.

She put her palms against his chest again, but she didn't shove him. Instead she ran her palms up until her arms linked around his neck. Then she pulled his head down and brushed her mouth across his.

The kiss took his breath away. It was gentle and loving and had hope swelling in Ronan's heart. Could she return his feelings?

He asked again, "What do you want, Muriel?"

"You," she said. "I want you..."

It wasn't a declaration of love. But it should have

been enough. It had always been enough for Ronan before. But then his heart had never been involved before.

He didn't want to wind up like his father—in love with a woman who didn't and probably couldn't love him back. But then he reminded himself that Muriel was not his mother.

She was straightforward and honest. And she had a heart—a big one—he'd seen it when she'd defended and supported her friend and when she'd interacted with the grandparents who raised her.

That was why he'd fallen for her. That and the incredible sex. Maybe he could make her fall for him— with incredible sex. He swung her up in his arms and headed toward his bedroom.

She wrapped her arm around his shoulders and snuggled into his neck, pressing kisses against his skin. He shuddered as passion overwhelmed him.

But when he stepped into his bedroom, he brought her to the bed, laid her down and stepped back. Her arms reached out for him, but he turned away and opened his closet door instead of joining her.

"What are you doing?" she asked, her voice thick with passion.

He pulled out four ties and held them up for her to see. "Letting you tie me up," he told her.

Her eyes widened in surprise. "Really?"

He nodded. "That way you'll know I won't run away afterward…"

"I told you I wouldn't try to tie you down anymore," she reminded him.

"I want to be tied down," he said, "with you."

He stripped off his clothes before knotting the end of each tie around one of the posts of his four-poster bed. Then he lay down on the king-size bed. "Tie me up," he invited her.

Muriel leaned over him, her beautiful face even more gorgeous with the big smile that curved up her full lips. "I love you."

The words hit him hard and made him hard, his cock swelling and extending toward her. He wanted to bury himself inside her—wanted to be so close that it wasn't possible to tell where one of them ended and the other began. But before he could reach for her, Muriel cinched a tie around his wrist. Then his other one and his ankles.

He had promised her this—had promised he'd give up control to her. But it was killing him. Then she was killing him with soft kisses and caresses…

With her lips and her fingertips, she touched every inch of his skin—in places he hadn't even realized he was sensitive. Like his knee and his hip…

He wanted to move, but he didn't fight the restraints. He didn't fight the feelings.

And when she closed her lips around his cock and sucked it deep into her mouth, he nearly came. But she just teased him, swirling her tongue around his girth. She even nibbled gently on the head.

He groaned. "Muriel, I want you... I want to be inside you..."

She pulled back and stared down at him. And for a moment, he wondered if this was it—her revenge. She was going to leave him tied up and out of his mind with passion and just walk away. But she'd said she loved him. Did she?

Muriel saw that fear flicker through Ronan's dark eyes again. And she knew he'd made himself more vulnerable to her than he had ever been.

His gorgeous body was naked and tethered to his bed. His cock pulsated with the need for release from the tension she'd built inside him.

But it was his heart that was most vulnerable— because, for the first time, Muriel could see it. Ronan's heart was in his gaze as he stared up at her. He didn't have to say the words she had. She knew. He loved her.

"I love you," she told him again.

And his body relaxed—slightly—and the fear passed out of his eyes, which warmed with that love she'd already seen. "I love you," he said.

He didn't have to tell her. She knew that was the first time he'd ever said those words to a woman. And she was so damn glad she was that woman.

His woman...

She pulled off her dress and dropped it to the floor on top of his clothes. She wore the lingerie she'd modeled last in the show. The silk and lace was purple and black and sexy as hell with bows holding it together in the back. She turned around, so he could see the bows as she tugged them loose.

Then the lingerie dropped to the floor—leaving her as naked as he was.

He struggled now against those restraints. "I want to touch you," he said, his voice gruff. "I have to touch you…"

And she needed his touch. She untied his silk power-tie bindings.

But when he was free, he didn't automatically reach for her. Instead, he studied her face. "You're not afraid I'm going to run off?"

She shook her head. "Not anymore…"

He leaned closer and kissed her lips. "I'm not going anywhere…"

"Well, this is your place," she reminded him.

He laughed and leaned his forehead against hers. "I love you."

Love rushed through her—along with desire. The power of both stunned her. "I hated you," she said, "after what you did to me in court and the media."

"I'm sorry," he said, his eyes darkening with regret. He lowered his head, as if unable to look at her. "I hate myself for what I did."

She slid her fingers along his hard jaw, tipping it back up so their gazes met. "That's all in the past now," she assured him. "Now I love you far more than I ever hated you…"

He expelled a ragged breath of relief. "That's good. I worried that you would never be able to forgive me."

She wrapped her arms around his neck and pressed her naked body against his. She felt his cock move between them, pulsating with desire. And her clit began to throb. She'd never wanted anyone more— not even Ronan himself.

Love changed everything, made every touch and kiss more intense. He kissed her deeply, and her toes nearly curled with the passion coursing through her.

Then he stroked his hands down her bare back to her hips and lifted her. She wrapped her legs around his waist and rubbed her clit against his penis. A moan tore free from her throat. She nearly came at just that contact. And she couldn't stop moving, couldn't stop shifting her hips against him.

"Muriel," he said on a groan. "You're going to make me…"

"Come!" she yelled as she shuddered and began to come herself. But it wasn't enough. She wanted more. She wanted him buried deep inside her.

And he must have wanted the same, for he quickly, despite his shaking hand, rolled on a condom. Then he rolled her across the bed, parted her legs and slid deep inside her.

Muriel clutched him to her, raking her nails down his back. The muscles rippled beneath her fingertips.

Then she grasped his butt. It was so tight, so firm...
so damn sexy.

"You really could be a model..." she murmured
against his lips as his mouth settled on hers.

He kissed her deeply, his mouth sliding over and
over hers. She parted her lips on a gasp of pleasure,
and he slid his tongue into her mouth. His cock slid
in and out of her, as well. She arched her hips, taking
him deeper and deeper.

But he rolled again, moving onto his back so that
she wound up on top. She moaned as his cock sank
even deeper. She was so close, the tension inside her
nearly unbearable. Ronan gripped her hips, lifting
her and moving her, as he arched his hips up from
the mattress. They found the rhythm that was theirs
alone—like a station on the radio that only the two
of them could hear.

And the tension broke as an orgasm overwhelmed
her. Her body shuddered as her inner muscles convulsed. She screamed as the orgasm went on and on
and on...

Ronan's hands tightened on her hips as his body
tensed beneath hers. Then he shouted her name as he
came. Muriel lifted herself off him and dropped onto
the bed next to him. But as usual, he moved quickly—
leaving her lying alone on the tangled silk sheets.

Maybe she shouldn't have untied him. But he was
back within seconds. He wrapped his arm around her,
pulling her against him.

She settled her head onto his chest. His heart was still beating fast and frantically beneath her ear. "Are you okay?" she asked.

His arm tightened for a moment. "I'm afraid," he admitted.

She'd thought he'd already made himself as vulnerable as he could be to her when he'd professed his love and then let her tie him up. But this was even bigger than that.

"Why are you afraid?" she asked.

"I've never felt like this before," he said. "It's overwhelming."

She pressed her lips against his chest. "I know. But I will never hurt you."

His heart beat slowed in pace and intensity. And his hand was steady as it skimmed down her back in a sweet caress. "I trust you," he said. "I just hope I don't screw this up. I don't want you to leave…"

"I'm not going anywhere," she assured him.

He must have believed her because eventually he fell asleep. And Muriel drifted off, as well.

But when she awoke a while later, panic flashed through her. Ronan was gone.

But he hadn't gone far. She felt his lips…on her ankle. Then silk replaced his mouth as he wrapped a tie around it. The other end was already tethered to the bedpost.

"What are you doing?" she asked.

"Tying you up," he said.

"Afraid I might run now?" she asked.

"Not at all," he said. "I'm not afraid of anything anymore."

"Then what are you doing?"

"Showing you how much I love you…"

He showed her over and over again as he kissed and caressed every inch of her. His lips touched her everywhere, the inside of her elbow, the curve of her hip, the back of her knee…

Then he dipped his tongue into her belly button before moving farther down her body. As he rubbed one of her nipples between his thumb and finger, he kissed her mound. Then he made love to it, stroking his tongue over her and nibbling at her with his lips.

She tugged against the restraints, wanting to touch him—wanting to drag him up her body, so that he could bury himself inside her.

But then she arched off the bed as an orgasm shuddered through her. He wasn't done, though. He kept making love to her with his mouth until she came again and again.

The sheets weren't just tangled but damp beneath her. When he finally released her, she launched herself at him. They made love in a frenzy, his cock sliding deep into her wetness.

She shuddered as she came again. "Ronan…" She nearly sobbed his name.

Then he tensed, his body going stiff before he drove deep with one last thrust. He shouted her name and dropped onto the mattress next to her. His skin was slick, like hers. "They got that title wrong," he murmured.

"Title?"

"The World's Most Beautiful Woman."

Unoffended, she brushed her sweat-soaked hair back from her face and wholeheartedly agreed, "I always thought they got it wrong, too."

"Your title should be…" He paused dramatically before continuing. "The World's Best Lover…"

She smiled and settled her head back against his shoulder. "That title is yours," she told him. "All yours…"

"It's ours," he corrected her. "We are amazing together."

But they were more than just lovers now. They were in love. And while her lover might be a little too cynical to totally believe it would last, she had no doubts. They had already survived the worst.

They had nothing but pleasure ahead of them.

* * * * *

LET'S TALK
Romance

For exclusive extracts, competitions
and special offers, find us online:

f facebook.com/millsandboon

⊙ @millsandboonuk

🐦 @millsandboon

Or get in touch on 0844 844 1351*

For all the latest titles coming soon, visit
millsandboon.co.uk/nextmonth